WITCH FOR HIRE

PARANORMAL TEMP AGENCY

MOLLY FITZ

Sweet Promise Press
PO Box 72
Brighton, MI 48116

ABOUT THIS BOOK

My name is Tawny Bigford. I'm 35, single, and I love hot showers. Seriously, all I wanted was a hot shower to start my day off right, but when I went to confront my landlady about the broken plumbing, I wound up talking to her corpse instead.

Now everyone thinks I'm to blame for her murder—not the best way to make an impression on the new neighbors, let me tell you. But how can I prove I'm innocent when I know practically nothing about the woman I supposedly killed?

Especially not the fact that she was the official Beech Grove Town Witch. Her former boss—a snarky black cat named Mr. Fluffikins—says I have to fill her vacated role until the real killer can be caught and brought to justice.

So, whether I like it or not, I've just been recruited to the Paranormal Temp Agency. Now I need to solve my landlady's murder, figure out how to wield my newly granted powers, and maybe even find a way to fit in around here.

Yup. All in a day's work for this novice witch.

AUTHOR'S NOTE

Hey, new reader friend!

Welcome to the crazy inner workings of my brain. I hope you'll find it a fun and exciting place to be.

If you love snarky talking animals and crazy magical mishaps as much as I do, then I'm pretty sure you're going to enjoy the journey ahead.

This book is just the first of many brain-tickling adventures to come, so make sure you keep in touch to keep in the know!

I've done my best to make it easy by offering several fun ways to access sneak peeks of upcoming books, monthly giveaways, adorable pictures of my own personal feline overlords, and many other cool things that are just for my inner circle of readers.

So take a quick moment now to choose your favorite:

Download my app
Join my VIP reader group
Sign up for my newsletter
Kick off a cat chat on Facebook

This is the first book in a brand-new series, and I hope you'll love it! The second is already available here, and my popular Pet Whisperer P.I. is 12 books and growing!

So enjoy **Witch for Hire,** snag your copy of **Psychic for Hire,** and then consider giving Pet Whisperer P.I. a try when you're done.

You can check out book 1, **Kitty Confidential,** or grab a **special boxed collection** of the first three books together. Either is a great place to start...

Okay, ready to talk to some animals and solve some mysteries?

Let's do this!

Molly Fitz

"Aaaaaaaaah!" A scream tore from my chest as I leaped away from the frigid stream gushing out of the old showerhead.

Normally I loved starting my mornings with a slow and steamy rinse while I let all of my thoughts boing around my brain and eventually meld themselves into some kind of plan for the day. Ever since moving to Beech Grove a couple weeks back, however, I was lucky to get a good five minutes of warmth before the water heater suddenly gave up the ghost and a punishing spray of liquid ice ruined my good mood.

"That's it!" I shouted as I twisted the faucet off. My landlady would be hearing from me today, whether she liked it or not.

For her part, old Mrs. Haberdash had given me very careful instructions when I signed up to rent the small guest home at the back edge of her hilltop property. Even though she lived in the main house, just a short walk away, I was never ever supposed to visit her there. Anything I needed could be explained via a phone call or better yet—*at least according to her*—an old-fashioned letter.

Yeah, no.

I tried to do it her way, but so far my attempts at getting help with the plumbing had gone unanswered, and unfortunately, a useless shower made for a useless me. I'd tried playing by her rules and still had nothing to show for it. Now it was a time to play by mine.

Still dripping, I bunched my soapy hair into a bun to get it off my shoulders, threw on a shift dress and flip-flops, and headed out to finally confront my apathetic landlady.

I guess now would be a good time to introduce myself.

The name's Tawny, Tawny Bigford. Tawny is short for *Tanya,* a name I've hated ever since Tanya Mills stuck a chewed-up wad of bubble gum in my hair during our second grade spelling test. So now I'm Tawny.

I'm 35, love my showers—as you already know—and am wonderfully, happily, unapologetically single.

Sure, I had a husband once. George was his name. But several years into our marriage, he decided he made a much better pair with some PTA mom named Patricia.

A PTA mom!

As the story goes, they'd bumped into each other outside of the local middle school one afternoon, and it was love at first sight. Why George was there in the first place, I'll never understand. It's not like we had kids of our own or any other reason for him to find himself at exactly the wrong place and wrong time.

But it happened and changed all of our lives in the process.

Honestly, I'd have rather he slipped off with his younger, prettier secretary. At least then I could bemoan the cliche.

But he and Patricia, who is two years his senior, are disgustingly happy together. Most days I just pretend that neither of them exists.

Okay, so I may sound *a little* bitter. And I may live by myself in a rented guest house, but—disappointing showers not withstanding—I absolutely love my life. Basically I write two books per year, ship them off to my publisher for a paycheck, and then do whatever I want with the rest of my time.

Yes, I could write more to make more, but why? I'm perfectly happy to live frugally because that means living freely. And as such, I have more hobbies than any one person should probably ever have.

But I digress...

This wasn't the time to discuss my hobbies, it was the time to confront Mrs. Haberdash and to demand a steady supply of hot water that lasted more than five minutes per day. It was, after all, a simple and basic necessity.

On her doorstep now, I sucked in a deep breath to calm my rage, raised my hand, and knocked gently.

Just kidding, I pounded on that door with every bit of ire I had in me.

When no one answered, I started to shout. "I know you're in there! And I need to talk!"

Still nothing, so I tried the doorknob and was surprised to find it unlocked, given how much I knew the woman valued her privacy.

I pushed it open and charged in, ready to give old Mrs. Haberdash a piece of my mind.

Unfortunately, while all this righteous storming was going on, I hadn't kept an eye on my feet. I hadn't thought I needed to, but something big and heavy was lying on the ground just beyond the threshold and I slammed right into it, lost my balance, and thudded to the ground in an awkward tangle of limbs.

Not just my own, but Mrs. Haberdash's, too. *Uh-oh.* My stomach churned with an aching certainty.

"M-M-Mrs. Haberdash?" I asked, my voice quavering with fright as I turned my face toward the old woman sprawled across the entryway floor.

Her mouth remained firmly closed, her eyes glued open, her body even colder than the shower I'd just escaped.

Yup, she was dead, and—thanks to my unfortunate stumble—I'd just gotten my DNA all over her corpse.

No, no, no! I attempted a scream but came up short.

And here I thought a cold shower was the absolute worst way to start the day. Oh, when would I ever learn to leave well enough alone?

scrambled away from Mrs. Haberdash's prone body in an awkward crab walk that sent an uncomfortable twinge tearing through my underworked arm muscles—because even though I had a lot of hobbies, none of them related to fitness.

"That's okay about the plumbing," I sputtered, despite knowing Mrs. Haberdash could neither hear me nor do anything about it now. "I'll just... Yeah. So bye for now."

I used the banister at the base of her grand staircase to pull myself to my feet, but before I could fully regain my composure, another horrible thing happened.

Law enforcement arrived.

"What's going on in here?" A tall man with thick salt-and-pepper hair and a light beard glanced from Mrs. Haberdash to me and back again, then picked up the radio attached to his belt and—

"Stop!" I cried, unsure of what to do with my hands. I ended up grabbing the banister with both hands, just to appear non-threatening.

The cop lowered his handheld and regarded me skeptically.

"What's going on here?" he asked again, his eyes fixed firmly on me now. They were a pale gray, the kind of eyes I would write into a character to show the reader he was handsome. And he was handsome, but unfortunately, I had a few more pressing things on my mind at the moment.

I looked incredibly guilty here. There was no denying that. In fact, I wouldn't be surprised if Officer Pretty Eyes pressed me up against the wall and started reading me my rights at that very moment. *Brain, stop freaking out!*

I needed to stop thinking about what could happen here and just focus on remaining calm and collected while I explained exactly why it was I'd wound up alone with a dead body.

"Well... I..." I fumbled for my words, sighed, and

began again. "I mean... Mrs. Haberdash is dead, so..."

Oh, c'mon, Tawny! If you can't use your writing superpowers to explain away something you didn't even do, what's the point of even having them?

I simpered at him uncomfortably, waiting for the guy to either arrest me or to tell me to be on my way. It didn't seem like there was much chance for an in-between here. I mean, *I* would have arrested me.

"Yes, dead. I can see that," he said, glancing toward her body demonstratively before snapping his gaze back to mine.

A jolt shot through me, but whether it was excitement, fear, or something else entirely, I couldn't quite tell.

"Why did you kill her?" he pressed, his eyes boring into mine as if trying to see straight into my thoughts.

"I didn't!" I stomped my foot for good measure. Maybe my body could say what my words could not. "This morning in the shower..."

He raised one suggestive eyebrow that sent flames straight into my cheeks. Why did he have to be so good looking? That made this whole situation so much worse. I'd always been great at writing banter, but not so great at actually doing it in real life. Besides, it's not like flirting could get me out of this one.

"No, not that. I mean, yes, the hot water," I back-pedaled again and then panicked when he reached back toward his belt. "Wait! I didn't kill her! How could you even think that?"

He crossed his arms and stared down the bridge of his nose at little old me. "How could I think that? Easy. I've never seen you a day in my life, not until you suddenly showed up at a murder scene."

I gasped in horror. "Murder? No, she wasn't murdered. I mean, at least not by me. And, hey, why do you automatically assume foul play? You've been here all of five seconds and have hardly even glanced at her. Don't you have to do like an investigation or something first?"

Ugh. Me and my big mouth!

First I couldn't defend my innocence, and then I accused him of not doing his job properly. I may have written one or two police characters in my books, but that wasn't quite enough to make me an expert here.

He groaned and shook his head. "Yes, and I will investigate, just as soon as I'm done questioning the suspect."

I backed up until my shoulders were pressed flat

against the wall. "Look, Deputy Quick Draw, Mrs. Haberdash is my landlady. I was just coming to lodge a complaint. A small one. Nothing to kill anyone over." I inserted a nervous laugh here as one does when a topic is quite literally *dead* serious.

"She was like this when I got here," I added as an afterthought.

"Looks like she's been here for a while," he said with a sniff.

"I don't know anything about any of this. I just wanted some hot water for my morning shower. That's all."

Gathering every last vestige of strength, I pushed off from the wall and carefully navigated around poor Mrs. Haberdash in a last-ditch effort to get the heck out of there.

The cop's light eyes roamed over me, and the slightest smile quirked on his lips.

"Hang on," he said, stopping me in my tracks as a heavy veil of horror dropped over me once again. "You're going to have to come with me."

Noooooooo!

3

Officer Quick Draw left me no time to argue. When I hesitated to follow him toward his squad car, he unhooked a pair of handcuffs from his belt loop and dangled them before me. "Would you prefer we give these babies a workout instead?"

Motivation had arrived. And just like that, I was power walking across my dead landlady's dead lawn and yanking open the passenger side door to throw myself inside.

The officer gave me a strange look, but I shrugged it off. "If I'm not under arrest, then I'm not riding in the back. I've lived in enough small towns to know how fast and far rumors can fly." Things couldn't get much worse at this point, so I had to fight for whatever small dignities I could retain. I'd already been driven out of my former hometown by the embarrassment of my ex-husband's indiscretion.

Since then, I'd briefly lived in two other small towns, but neither felt quite right. I'd been hoping Beech Grove would finally offer a new place to put down roots, but that was probably ruined now. Still, I'd rather whatever time I had here be as pleasant as possible.

I glanced back at Mrs. Haberdash's dark, imposing house. It looked like the kind of place where murders happened. Why hadn't I seen that before?

The cop slammed his door, jabbed his key into the ignition, and chuckled as the engine rumbled to life. "So you're new."

I nodded in confirmation. "And I'm guessing you're not."

"Born and raised right here in Beech Grove," he admitted with a faint blush. "It's all I've ever known. What I don't know is your name. You still haven't told me that little piece of info." He smiled to himself as he maneuvered the squad car with me in it. It would have been easy to like him under other circumstances, but now he would forever be the guy who took me in for murder.

I offered a sarcastic laugh to hide my discomfort. "It's kind of hard to introduce oneself when one's companion is hurling murder accusations around like they were *Mardi Gras* beads."

"Oneself, eh? *Smart.* You a new professor at the academy, then?" We'd already pulled out of the driveway and were rumbling down the torn-up back road. He did glance at me briefly as if making some kind of assessment.

"What academy?" We were at least an hour away from any kind of big city. Seemed a weird place for something as fancy as an academy.

He frowned but didn't clarify. "How about we try starting over here? Hi. I'm Parker Barnes. It's nice to meet you."

I kept my eyes fixed firmly ahead and nodded.

"And you are?" Parker prompted after several silent moments passed.

"Tawny," I answered even though I really didn't want to.

"*There.* Now that wasn't so hard, was it?"

I shook my head and let out a beleaguered sigh. "I'd really rather not make chit-chat with some guy who thinks I killed my landlady. Let's just get the questioning over with and go on our separate ways. Okay?"

"Touché, madame. Lucky for you, we're already there."

The car jerked to a stop, shocking me with how short this journey had been.

I widened my eyes at the sight of the sprawling brick building before us. It wasn't just a single building, but a whole complex—and it definitely wasn't a police station. I didn't remember ever passing it before on my walks through town, either. Though it obviously wasn't far from where I lived, judging from the short time between climbing into this cruiser and reaching our destination.

"I thought you were taking me to the station?" I said, crossing my arms across my chest in open defiance.

"This is the station, at least for our purposes today. C'mon. We've lost too much time already."

I turned to stare at him. He didn't look like your garden variety murderer-rapist-all-around-psycho, but that didn't mean he wasn't. I refused to follow him blindly just because he wore a uniform. Uniforms could be faked, after all.

"Everything only *just* happened. How have we lost time?" I demanded, sitting firm. "And, no, I know better than to go into a strange building with a strange man. I'm staying right here." Not that camping out in his strange car was any better, but still, a girl had to stand up for herself—otherwise who would?

"Okay, but if anyone asks, you're the one who chose to do this the hard way," Parker answered with yet another frown before exiting the car.

I watched as he marched around the car, came to my side, and then flung the door open. "Out," he said firmly.

I opened my mouth to argue but let out a scream instead. My hands were moving to unbuckle the seatbelt, my feet to pull me from the car. I had told neither of them to do those things. "Hey," I cried in a pathetic protest. "Stop it."

"Follow me," Parker said, obvious enjoyment now dancing in his light eyes.

My legs answered as if they belonged to him instead of me. The no-good traitors.

And into the unmarked office in the non-police building I went, thanks to my frighteningly bossy companion and inexplicably disobedient limbs.

Yup, this day just kept on getting worse and worse.

And that definitely didn't bode well for whatever happened next.

4

We entered a chilly office space that sat dark and dim despite how brightly the late morning sun shone outside. Okay, so I might have slept in a little that day, but I was between books so it didn't really matter.

"Your instincts were bang on," Parker said to someone I couldn't see. "Haberdash is dead. And I found this one at the scene."

"Well, that doesn't bode well for the rest of the day," a smooth voice responded from somewhere deeper inside. Each of his words rolled directly into the next without taking any small breaks for breath. I'd almost describe it as serpentine, although that description wasn't exactly right, either.

More than a little intrigued, I whipped my head

from side to side but still couldn't locate the speaker. "Who's there? What do you want with me?"

The disembodied voice chuckled, and I thought I caught a glimpse of movement at the edge of the room, but just as quickly as I spotted it, the dark form had slunk back into the even darker shadows.

"Well, that certainly isn't good. Take her to the conference room," the voice instructed in that same overly polished manner. "I'll summon the others."

Parker placed a hand at the small of my back, and I wriggled away from him. "Don't touch me," I snapped.

"Sorry," he said, seeming genuinely apologetic. He cleared his throat before speaking again. "Follow me. Um, please."

My legs snapped into action, despite my mind screaming for them to stop, turn around, and run as fast as I could out the door.

I was a lifeless marionette in his hands, little Pinocchio before the fairy godmother brought him to life.

We walked down one hall, turned, and then walked to the end of another that opened into a large meeting room with a glass ceiling. I'd have been impressed if I weren't already equal parts agitated and terrified.

"What do you want with me?" I demanded, searching Parker's eyes, hoping that with the right expression I could convince him to let me go before any serious damage was done.

"Have a seat," he said with what seemed like a sad shake of his head. I wasn't buying that. If he was so sad about this, then he wouldn't have kidnapped me in the first place.

My hands moved to grip the nearest chair and pull it back.

"You don't have to," Parker said suddenly, and my hands fell limply to my sides. "Unless you want to."

"I'd rather stand," I managed through gritted teeth. "Actually I'd rather go."

I started toward the door.

"No!" he cried, and I froze in place. "I'm sorry. I know you must have a million questions, and you'll get answers for all of them. Well, most at least. We just have to wait for—"

The door flew open and four people marched in, glancing briefly in my direction as they assembled themselves around the table. Most were much older than me or Parker. At least one of them looked like he was mere days away from celebrating his one-hundredth birthday. A long white beard hung limply against his chest, making him look a bit like Merlin in a business suit. Why would a one-hundred-year-old man need a business suit, and why would he be wearing it now? These were but a few of the many questions flying through my mind as I studied the new arrivals.

I had just peeked under the table to check out the footwear of a particularly well-dressed woman who appeared to be in her late fifties or early sixties when a black cat trotted through the doorway and leaped up onto the table in one graceful, confident pounce.

"Now that we're all here," the voice I'd heard in the outer room began.

Of course, I didn't hear what he said next, because an internal scream took over my brain as I realized that same smooth voice was coming from the cat. *The cat!*

And it's not just that the cat was talking—he seemed to be in charge, too.

He placed one paw directly in front of the other and sauntered across the table, his glowing yellow eyes fixed right on me. "Well?"

"Well, wh-what?" I stuttered. I also struggled and strained, but nothing I tried released my legs back into my control.

"Are you the one who killed her?" The words

danced out from the cat's mouth, and I realized now why it sounded so strange. He didn't need his tongue to form the sounds. That removed a lot of the wet breathiness out of speech.

"No answer," he said thoughtfully. "Does that mean you plead guilty?"

"No!" I shouted. "Now let me go!"

The cat turned to Parker and waited.

The once-confident police officer appeared frazzled in the company of the demanding feline. "She was there when I arrived. I thought we could—"

"Make use of her until we find out who really did it. Provided it's not actually she who committed the deed, of course. Brilliant idea, Barnes." The black cat strolled back to the head of the table, and the people seated on either side murmured their agreement.

I still had no idea what was going on, but at least now I knew they didn't plan to kill me. "Excuse me," I piped up. "Make use of me how?"

"Oh, you'll see soon enough," the cat promised with a rather unfriendly chuckle.

With that, Parker rose from his seat and strode toward me with one hand extended as he shot me an uneasy smile.

The others rose from their chairs, too, and

formed a line behind him, waiting for their turn to greet me themselves, apparently.

When I hesitantly returned Parker's handshake, he said, "Welcome to the Paranormal Temp Agency. You're hired!"

What? How could I be hired when I hadn't even applied for a job?

Also, there was the small fact that I was most definitely not a paranormal person. I was normal with a capital *N,* and I didn't like what was happening here one bit.

5

I'd just discovered a murder, been kidnapped, and then offered a job by a talking cat. How much weirder could this day get?

I shook my head vehemently. "Sorry, I already have a job."

"It's not up for debate," the cat hissed back at me. "Get her up to speed and fast, Barnes. My patience here is wearing thin."

"Okay. Okay. Where to begin?" Officer Parker Barnes wondered aloud while I was left to wonder if he really was a police officer or if it had all been a ruse from the start.

"This time, you probably want to be sitting down," he said, pulling out a chair for me.

I crossed my arms over my chest and stood firm. "I managed to survive the talking cat without passing out. I think I can handle whatever you're going to say next."

"Suit yourself." He chuckled, but I thought I saw a flicker of respect cross his face. "Lila Haberdash was Beech Grove's Town Witch, and now that she's dead the position is open. In the meanwhile, it's yours."

"Uh-huh, uh-huh." I nodded my head adamantly. "There's just one problem with that."

"You're not a witch?" Parker asked with one eyebrow quirked.

"I'm not a witch!" I shouted in confirmation, wringing my hands as I did. "So, thanks but no thanks. I'll just be on my way."

"Enough with this game already," the cat snapped. "If you can't handle her, I'll just have to take over. Come here!"

I raced to his side against my own volition. I was really getting sick of all this mind control stuff.

The cat lifted his nose high in the air, leaving me with a perfect view of the small white patch at the top of his chest. Normally, I liked cats. Not enough to own one, mind you, but I liked them well enough when they were other people's pets. This one, however, had recently risen to the top of my list of people—um, creatures—I didn't much care for.

"You've been hired on to the Paranormal Temp Agency," he told me with a twitch of his nose and a flick of his tail. "It's not a job you're allowed to turn down."

"I think I know what I'm allow—"

"Stop arguing and listen. You *will* fill Lila's old post as Town Witch until we're able to uncover her actual killer to take on the role permanently. None of this is up for debate."

"Why does finding the killer matter? Can't you just put up a job advertisement on Spooks R Us or something?"

"Cute," he said with a scowl. "You're filling in for Lila, whether you like it or not. Help us find the murderer, and you'll be off the hook sooner. End of story."

Parker cleared his throat, then explained the part that still confused me most. "Magic passes to the nearest host when its original owner passes. So whoever killed Lila likely absorbed her magic—a magic which is grounded in Beech Grove and is meant for its designated witch."

I stood still, considering this. Parker's explanation made sense, but it also begged so many new questions. Mainly, what would have happened if no one else had been around? What if Mrs. Haberdash had died of natural causes and then her magic had found its way over to me, the sole resident of the guest house on the edge of her property?

I still didn't like that I was expected to help clean up this mess when it had nothing to do with me. I felt sad for Mrs. Haberdash, of course. Even though she wasn't a great landlady, she hadn't deserved to be murdered. But I also didn't deserve to be put in harm's way, especially if the person who'd offed Haberdash decided to come for me next.

Maybe I still had a quick and easy way out of this, though. I raised my hand and pointed at the cat.

"Come to me," I said, trying to push power into the simple command, the way I'd seen both the cop and the cat do.

Boss cat rolled his eyes. "Should I take this feeble attempt at magic as your confession of guilt?"

"No," I mumbled as embarrassment burned at my cheeks.

"Even if you do have magic, which at this point I sincerely doubt, you still aren't strong enough to command me. No one is. That's why I'm the boss, and you're the temp. Got it?"

"Whatever," I answered drolly. "So I don't have magic. That should be the end of this conversation, then. How can I fill in as the Town Witch without having any magic? Clearly, you've got the wrong woman here."

"You'll be granted everything you need to perform your duties, including some temporary magic."

I bit back an argument. There was a lot wrong with this scenario, but also... *I'd just been offered magic!* How could I possibly say no to that?

"Fine," I stated with a shrug instead. "Then I guess I accept. Can I please have my magic now?"

"Tonight at orientation. Eleven o'clock sharp."

"Sorry, I sleep at night."

"Not anymore you don't." The cat turned away from me with an irritated flick of his tail and faced the rest of his board. "Disperse."

Everyone left except for Parker and me.

"Sorry to drag you into all this," he said. "But take it from someone who knows, don't mess with Mr. Fluffikins so much. Your life will be much easier if you show him some respect."

I burst out laughing, but Parker only looked afraid.

Seriously though, what could a little black cat named Mr. Fluffikins even really do to me?

Unfortunately, I'd find out later that night.

6

*A*fter Parker dropped me off back home, I finally finished the shower I'd started what felt like a lifetime ago. Yes, it was still uncomfortably cold, but that discomfort helped me work some of the shock out of my bones. Actually, it was just what I needed.

As I toweled off, I made a mental catalog of the things I knew:

My landlady was a witch.

She'd been murdered.

Her killer was still out there.

Now I was expected to fill her emptied shoes.

That night I'd be given temporary magic.

And my boss was a talking cat.

I wrote fiction for a living—telling stories was my

literal job—and still I couldn't have come up with something quite this crazy, even if I'd tried.

In fact, if it had been up to me, I'd have chosen a much more worthy heroine to take my place, and instead of a jerky cat, I'd probably have written Parker into the authoritative role. It would make for an interesting office romance premise. Opposites attract, enemies to lovers... Yeah, it checked all the boxes for the makings of a good book.

Still, I guess that's why people liked to say that life was stranger than fiction.

First that harlot of a PTA mom, and now this. What a riveting life I led.

Fully dried off now, I slipped into my favorite pair of jeans and an old T-shirt, then pulled on my running shoes. Did I ever run? No, don't be silly. But it made me feel like I could if I had to, wearing shoes meant for that purpose.

Then again, if things went south with my training tonight, I might actually have to put the poor sneakers to use for the first time in their miserable lives. I shuddered. *Best not to think about that.*

Suited up in my inconspicuous casual wear, I headed outside and crept down the worn path to my former landlady's main residence.

Imagine my surprise when I found I wasn't the only one who'd had that idea.

A young woman wearing a black maxi dress with a floral printed cardigan, scuffed up combat boots, and a big floppy sunhat stood in front of the house staring up at a second-floor window. She was so immersed in her inspection that she didn't seem to notice me approaching.

I hesitated. Would it be better if I turned back and pretended this whole thing had never happened?

It was too late for that, I supposed. I was a part of this now, whether I liked it or not.

And so, I raised my hand in greeting and shouted, "Hello there!"

The other woman startled so badly, she somehow managed to dislodge her hat, which the wind immediately swept up in a sudden playful gust.

We both ran after it, but a high up tree branch claimed it before either of us even had a chance.

The stranger bit her lip and turned toward me. "That was my favorite hat."

"That was my favorite landlady," I said, deciding just to jump into it as I motioned toward the now vacant house. "Did you know her well?"

"Not really," the woman said with one last

lingering glance toward her lost hat. Now that her face was fully exposed, I could tell she was even younger than I'd originally guessed. I wouldn't be surprised if she'd only just finished high school in the last year or two.

"I'm Tawny," I offered with a warm smile. "And you are?"

"Nobody important," she mumbled with another glance toward her lost sun hat. Her long black tresses blew in the breeze, giving her an almost ghastly appearance. "I really should be on my way."

"Wait," I cried, not entirely sure how I meant to follow that up. But I couldn't just let her get away. What if she was the murderer? I owed it to my former landlady to find out.

"What are you doing here?" I demanded when she turned back to me with a resigned sigh. "Did you know Mrs. Haberdash was murdered?"

Her eyes bore into mine, direct and determined but also giving nothing away. I suddenly became very aware that I had confronted someone who could be lethally dangerous. *Was* this the killer? Did she have the magic that belonged to the town?

When she didn't answer, I took a guess. "You did. Didn't you? Know she was killed, I mean. But do you know why someone would want her dead?"

"It was a mistake coming here," she spat, then turned on her heel and strode off so quickly I didn't have a prayer of catching her despite having donned my running shoes.

"Wait," I called after her again, but that nameless girl didn't acknowledge me and didn't turn back.

Well, shoot.

I'd had the suspect right here but hadn't been able to get anything useful out of her. If she'd been a friend or family member, she'd have said something, right? Her sudden departure screamed of a guilty conscience—but could she be guilty of murder?

Whatever the case, I had a feeling this strange visitor would turn up again sooner rather than later. Hopefully, though, it wouldn't be with murderous intent, especially now that she knew I suspected her.

Gah!

What was wrong with me? I hadn't merely tiptoed around danger, I'd dived headfirst in after it.

$\mathcal{I}$ spent the rest of that day trying and failing to write some pages to make my agent happy. Of course I had way too much on my mind to focus, which meant my agent would just have to get used to being unhappy with me for a while.

Parker turned up outside my cottage at fifteen minutes to eleven that night. Apparently he was my official keeper when it came to all things Paranormal Temp Agency.

And even though I didn't feel I needed a constant chaperone, I was grateful that at least it was him. I mean, he had less sass than the cat. And he wasn't so bad on the eyes, either.

The old me would have leaned into that attraction a little, flirted whenever the moment felt right. But this was the new me, a woman who I was quite frankly still getting to know.

Ever since I stumbled over Mrs. Haberdash's dead body and straight into this brave new world full of strange magic, I'd been changed. Sure, it had happened just this morning, but both of these once-in-a-lifetime occurrences together made for a monumental shift in what I knew about myself and the greater world around me.

I strode out to Parker's car, wearing a confidence I didn't quite feel. I also wore a flowy black floor-length skirt with a tight black leather bustier, old boots which were mostly hidden beneath the skirt, and my favorite statement piece of jewelry—a shiny black metal necklace with a series of interesting shapes that kind of looked like an eagle if you squinted a bit.

Apparently I'd also shown up with more cleavage than my escort had anticipated. He turned beet red under that beard of his the moment his eyes locked onto said cleavage.

"You didn't have to get dressed up for this," he muttered, clenching his hands even tighter around the steering wheel.

"Is that your way of saying I look nice?" I teased. Okay, maybe the old me was still in there a little bit.

Parker coughed. "Sure. Let's go with *nice*. Um, did you have a good day?"

"I don't think there's much recovering from a murder accusation and the discovery of magic, so let's just call today *interesting* instead."

"We know you probably didn't kill her if that helps," he offered with an apologetic shrug.

Oh, good. They knew I *probably* wasn't guilty, which meant I wasn't fully in the clear yet. It also meant... "So I guess you didn't catch the real killer yet," I said with a sigh.

"No, but we have some leads." Parker's expression remained firm, serious.

Me, on the other hand, I preferred to lighten the mood a bit—especially when I was already feeling scared out of my mind. "So, what are you? Are you actually a cop, or was all that pomp and circumstance this morning simply for my benefit?"

I expected him to loosen up some at my playful banter, but no dice. He adjusted himself in his seat, sitting taller, commanding even more of a presence. His jaw clenched, and his shoulders tightened. Was he afraid of me, or just not good with people in general?

"I am an officer of the law, yes," he said, his voice deeper than usual. "I'm also the paranormal liaison to the force."

"So you're a double cop?" I asked, scrunching up my nose playfully.

Finally a smile spread across his face. "Something like that, yes."

"And the cat's your boss. What about all the other people who were there this morning?" If anyone was going to give me information, it would be Parker, so I decided to press him for all I could on the drive over. It would be easier to influence him privately without the watchful eyes of Mr. Fluffikins.

He glanced at me for a moment and the car jerked toward the curb. Maybe expecting him to multi-task behind the wheel wasn't the best idea I'd had that day.

Parker returned his attention to the road. "You mean, the other liaisons. Right?"

"If that's who was sitting around that conference room table, then yeah." I thought back to the woman with the fantastic outfit and the ancient guy with the Merlin beard and business suit. The other two had made less of an impression on me, but whoever they were, they were important enough to be at that meeting, which meant I shouldn't simply forget they existed.

Parker nodded and readjusted his hands on the wheel. "Yes, we're all liaisons. I'm the liaison to the police force. Each of them keep an eye on other key influencing bodies around the region."

I bit my lip to keep from frowning. I was beginning to feel stupid, considering how little I knew, and I hated nothing more than feeling stupid. "That's pretty vague. Are you saying you speak up for the paranormal interests with the police?"

The car jerked as Parker suddenly hit the brake —whether accidentally or on purpose, I couldn't quite tell. He eased off before we came to a full stop. Luckily, no one had been driving behind us, or we'd both have a serious case of whiplash right now.

Parker's voice turned pitchy and panicked. "No, no. Gosh, no. Non-magic people don't know anything about us, so there's definitely no speaking up about anything. We watch to protect us from them. Not the other way around."

The fact that he was so nervous had to mean I was hitting on all the good questions, right? I decided to keep going, even though I was more than a little concerned for my safety with such a reactive driver behind the wheel. "Uh, hello. I'm non-magic, but you wasted no time in showing your hand to me."

"You showed up at the murder scene for one of our most important magical locals, so yeah. We had no choice but to bring you in. Besides, you'll have some magic in you before the night is through."

A shiver of excitement passed through me. I was about to get magic. That almost made the whole being a murder suspect thing worthwhile.

Almost.

8

*T*he drive over was short and bumpy, thanks to Parker's erratic behavior behind the wheel. This time I was actually happy to see the dark office complex, because it meant we had made it to our location without the epic car crash I'd half-anticipated.

Inside Paranormal HQ, Parker guided me in the opposite direction we'd gone that morning. A series of long halls delivered us to a large, echoing space where all the furniture had been cleared away and the carpeting ripped out.

"You're definitely not getting the security deposit back on this place," I mumbled, remembering the time I'd forfeited one of my own, thanks to an ill-fated attempt at candle making. Incidentally, that was not a hobby I'd decided to keep.

I turned toward Parker to see how my joke had gone over, but before I could meet his eyes, we were joined by a new arrival.

Mr. Fluffikins hopped down from a hole in the ceiling where one of the hanging tiles had been removed. He landed with a thump right in front of me, proving definitively—at least to me—that cats always landed on their feet.

"Good evening," he purred, appearing rather pleased with himself, if not with me.

"Thanks for bringing her to me, Barnes," he said, offering Parker a curt nod. "That will be all. Dismissed."

"Wait," I called after his departing form, but either he didn't hear me or he didn't care.

I glanced back toward the black cat with growing discomfort. Something told me he wouldn't be gentle in making my big introduction to magic.

"Human," he said, flicking the tip of his tail rhythmically as he regarded me. "It is time to—"

"My name's Tawny," I informed him.

His eyes widened as if my speaking my name had somehow been an insult. "That's not important. What's important is that—"

"Actually, my name is kind of important, and I'll thank you to use it." If I didn't put some rules in place now, I doubted I'd be able to introduce them later. And if I was going to be around long enough to do this Town Witch thing right, then I definitely needed to at least push for him to use my actual name.

Mr. Fluffikins rose to all four feet and paced a circle around me. "That's a rather tall demand from someone who still hasn't been cleared of murder."

"Actually it's a fairly simple request. You're asking me to learn magic and temporarily fill in for a witch. All I'm asking is that you treat me with a little respect."

The cat stopped, cocked his head to the side, and watched me with swirling golden eyes.

We both remained silent, unwilling to budge. As far as I was concerned, I had more leverage here. He may have magic, but he also needed me—and it had to be me for some reason, even though I had no idea why.

After what felt like a small eternity, the cat finally laughed. Not just a small chuckle, but a side-splitting display of amusement.

"You won't go easy on me, I see. I hope you know I'll extend you that same courtesy. So *Tawny* it is, but keep in mind, your future demands will be met with far more resistance."

"Thank you," I said between clenched teeth. Even though he'd finally given in, I still felt on edge. Why couldn't Parker have stayed with us? It would have been so much easier, having a friendly face along for the ride, even if he, too, was still largely a stranger. But I'd take the handsome cop over the scary magic cat any day of the week.

"So what now?" I asked when Mr. Fluffikins didn't make any effort to explain himself.

"Well, now," he said, while studying the unsheathed claws on one of his front paws. "Now I grant you temporary access to magic."

"Magic," I repeated, relishing the power of the word on my tongue.

The black cat nodded and schlinked those claws back into his paw. "It won't be a perfect match for Lila's, but it will be a fair replica and should allow you to temporarily fill her post. That is, unless you actually did kill her and have already absorbed her magical legacy."

"I didn't—" I was promptly cut off by a strong gust of wind that tore through the room and knocked me off my feet.

Ouchy ouch ouch. Everything hurt. My head, my chest, and especially my butt.

"What was that?" I screamed. He wanted me—needed me—to help him, right? So why was he attacking me all of a sudden?

Mr. Fluffikins opened his mouth, but instead of answering my very reasonable question, he unleashed a pulsing plume of fire.

It whipped out fast and determined, flying toward me much faster than I could ever hope to move even if I wasn't already knocked flat on my rear.

Then in a split instant, the flame disappeared, right before crashing into my face and turning me into a melted ball of wax.

"You're crazy!" I shouted, but fear made my words sound jumbled and drunken. "Let me out of here!"

Fluffikins laughed as he took slow deliberate steps in my direction. I took a deep breath and braced myself for whatever came next. We both knew I didn't have a snowball's chance in Miami of coming out the victor here.

But, oh, what a way to die!

9

"*R*elax," Fluffikins drawled as he stepped closer and closer.

Instantly my muscles loosened, and a calming thrum reverberated through my core.

The magical cat watched me for a moment.

When he decided I had well and truly followed his order, he continued with his horrifying presentation. "I had to make sure you didn't already have magic that you were attempting to hide. I can tell you don't have much practice, which means you wouldn't have been able to prevent yourself from unleashing your defenses at the sudden arrival of an external threat."

"You're crazy," I spat again. My body was calm, but my mind still reeled. "I don't have any magic, and I definitely don't appreciate you trying to turn me into roast Tawny!"

A smile stretched from one of his whiskered cheeks to the other. "Trusting a human with magic is no small thing. Your kind doesn't exactly have the best track record when it comes to wielding power of any kind."

Well, he had me there. Still, he may have understood humans, but that didn't mean he knew *me*.

"Don't attack me again," I ordered, wishing I already had the magic so I could force him to obey my command the same way he'd forced me to be calm.

"I hadn't planned on it. Now wait there." He crouched into a low pounce and then leaped into the same hole in the ceiling from which he'd emerged earlier.

Fluffikins was an unnaturally gifted jumper, that was for sure. *Oh, right. Magic, duh.*

When he returned, he had a simple silver brooch clutched in his mouth. It looked like a cross between a butterfly and a bow and appeared to be made of gleaming silver. He dropped it at my feet. "Your choice of attire isn't exactly suitable," he said in that off-putting almost serpentine way of his.

I glowered at Fluffikins. He may be the boss here,

but that didn't give him the right to control every aspect of my life. His latest barb stung, especially since I'd put so much effort into looking nice.

"No more insults," I growled.

But he didn't back down. Instead he buckled down. "It's just you have so much skin exposed. This is your magical badge." He placed a paw on the silver brooch. "It needs to be placed close to your heart to have the best effect."

I glanced down at my expansive cleavage and grimaced. "Oh, I see. *Hmmmm.*"

"Could you maybe just...?" His words fell away and, well, if you've never seen a black cat blush, I promise it's a sight to behold. Fluffikins coughed, which turned into a hack, which soon resulted in a slimy hairball being spat up right by my feet. Charming.

I grabbed the gleaming brooch, trying my best to not look at the mess that sat dangerously close. "How's this?" I asked after popping it at the very top of my bustier so it jutted slightly above the neckline.

"Well, let's put it to the tests." Fluffikins regained his composure, winked, then threw another gust of wind my way.

This time I raised both hands in front of me, and the wind immediately died down without so much as ruffling a single hair on my head. Shocked, I studied my hands in search of the magic which had just come out of them. They still looked—and felt—exactly the same.

I didn't have much time to think about it, though, because next came the fire. Instinctively, I thrust my hands forward and pushed out a stream of water that collided with Fluffikins's flames, causing both to blink out of existence.

The cat wore a smug expression now. "See. You can't help but defend yourself."

"But how? I definitely didn't do any of that on purpose." I continue to study my hands carefully as if they'd suddenly reveal all the secrets of the universe. Unfortunately, I still felt just as confused as ever—and possibly more.

"Wielding magic is as easy and natural as breathing air for those who have it. Yes, you must practice to strengthen it, but our natural aptitudes are innate within us."

"But I don't naturally have magic. I shouldn't have been able to do the things I just did," I argued. I didn't write fantasy, but I'd read enough of it to know that magic required lots of practice and self-control. This thing with Fluffikins tonight was turning out to be the exact opposite.

He shrugged as if none of this meant anything to him. "Everyone has the potential. Few just ever realize it's there."

"So every single person in the whole entire world has magic?" I marveled at this. How could such a big thing be kept a secret? Was it because of people like Parker and Fluffikins and all the other paranormal liaisons around the world? Was I part of that now? *Wow.*

"When it comes to adult humans, it's less than a fraction of a percent," Fluffikins informed me with a contented grin. "Most are too caught up with the other aspects of their busy lives."

"You said adults," I pointed out as I finally pulled myself to my feet. "Does that mean—?"

"Yes, many children can still access their innate magic, but as they grow older, the adults in their lives convince them it isn't real, and eventually most will lose that spark."

"That's actually really sad," I choked out.

"We already have more than enough messes to clean up from the few humans who keep their magic. Why do you think there are so many stray cats around? It's our job to keep an eye on you and fix things before the other humans realize they're broken."

"So stray cats are...?"

"Field agents, yes. If you ever have any extra money laying around, try to donate to your local shelters. We've lost too many good agents to..." He shuddered. "Never mind."

"I'll do what I can," I promised, wondering whether it would be okay to pet him or if such a gesture would be more condescending than comforting. "So what now?"

"Now, you head home and get some rest. I'll come for you in the morning to get you started on your Town Witch duties."

I wanted to thank him, to apologize for the friends he'd lost in the field, but before I could say anything, he raised his voice and bellowed, "Barnes!"

Parker appeared almost immediately, grabbed me by the arm, and led me away. Well, it looked like I'd have to wait for tomorrow to get any more answers.

10

I knew I should try to get some sleep, but I was way too excited to make such a thing possible. I still had so many new questions spinning about my brain, and they needed answers.

Of course, Parker had remained relatively tight-lipped on the drive back home, which left me to my own internal musings.

One thought in particular dominated my mind from the get-go: "OH MY GOSH, I HAVE MAGIC NOW! WHEEEEEE!"

Eager to put my new powers to the test once I was home, I tromped outside and stood in the yard, hoping for some violent winds I could silence... But the night remained calm, still, and highly uncooper-ative. I briefly considered setting up a campfire to douse with whatever decided to fly forth from my hands. Then again, who said my abilities were limited to soothing the elements? Both Parker and Fluffikins had worked some form of mind control on me, and even though I didn't have anyone to influence with me now, I bet I could do almost anything I set my mind to.

Let's see...

Fluffikins had pulled the magic out of me easily without either of us having to think much about it, but now that I was left to my own devices I didn't really know where to start.

I studied the brooch affixed to my top as if it would flash the answer in big bold letters. Nope, no such luck.

I still didn't even know what my new job as a Town Witch temp entailed. What would my responsibilities be? What kind of magic would I be able to perform? Fluffikins had offered precious little by way of explanation.

Luckily, as an author by trade, I was already well accustomed to indulging my imagination. True, I mostly wrote contemporary romance set in the real world—you know, the world that up until today I'd assumed had no magic. Usually when I wrote my books, I dreamed up cute ways for the heroines to meet their heroes or huge romantic gestures for the heroes to use to win back the heroines after messing things up royally. And while I was really good at doing both those things, neither helped in exploring my newly granted paranormal abilities.

Maybe if I wanted to cast a love spell or something... Wait, was that a thing I could actually do now? My breath hitched as I realized just how endless the possibilities might be.

This, of course, made me wonder how much of the common lore surrounding witches was based on reality and how much was simply the work of overactive imaginations like mine.

I ran through the ways I'd seen witches portrayed in the popular media.

Black cat familiar? *Check.*

Green and ugly? *Heck no.* I mean, at least not green and probably not ugly, either.

Fancy spell book? *Not yet.*

A flying broom? *Wait a sec...*

Would I really be able to fly? And if so, would I need a broom?

Yes, flying, was definitely going on the to-do list.

I was half-tempted to try it now by jumping off my roof and letting those survival instincts kick in like they had with Fluffikins, but that didn't seem like the smartest stunt to pull when I had no one around to magic up some healing or call an ambulance in case it all went wrong.

Flying would definitely have to wait...

But what else could witches do?

Hmmm. Maybe I could shape shift. I mean, why not?

Determined to find something I could do on my own, I headed to the one tiny bathroom in my rental cottage, placed both hands on the counter, and stared at myself in the mirror.

Let's see. Let's see. What could I shift into?

My eyes locked on the shower curtain with its bright pink flamingo print, the one item infused with any personality in this functional but not exactly appealing room.

A flamingo, okay. I pictured the bird in my mind, cataloging everything I knew about them from their flamboyantly colored feathers right down to their preference for standing on just one foot at a time. Squeezing my eyes shut, I held the image in my mind and pictured myself becoming that image.

Just. Think. Pink.

It was a perfectly logical method, and I gave the visualization thing all I had... But still nothing happened.

Darn it!

I opened my eyes again, ready to tell off my reflection for her refusal to follow instructions. Instead, I let out a sharp gasp.

I hadn't turned into a flamingo, but my hair *had changed* into a bright bubblegum pink that matched the color of the birds on the shower curtain perfectly.

Pink hair. I'd done that with magic—my magic!—and it didn't look half bad, considering.

Granted, I still didn't know how I'd managed to change just my hair when I'd meant to change my whole body, but I was thrilled I had done something. Even if it was just a small something.

I revisited my earlier list.

Green? *No.*

Ugly? *Not with this cool new hairdo.*

Yes, I'd harnessed my new powers and done something magical. Not a bad start at all for this novice witch. Whatever this Town Witch thing entailed, I could do it.

And who knew? Maybe I could tackle flying tomorrow.

Famous last words.

11

The next morning, a horrible screeching sound wrested me from an already fitful sleep. I bolted upright, pushing my back against the antique headboard and sending a certain black cat tumbling from the bed.

"What are you doing here?" I cried, clutching the comforter to my chest.

Mr. Fluffikins hopped back onto the foot of my bed and eyed me wearily. "I already told you we'd be picking up with your training this morning."

"But it's still dark outside." I knew I was whining like a child who'd just been woken up for the first day of school after an especially satisfying Christmas break, but I didn't care. I was too angry to worry about how I was coming across to the very person—*er,* cat—who had gotten me so angry to begin with. "Plus you said nothing about breaking into my house. That is not okay."

He squinted his eyes and growled, then straightened back up, proud and tall, showing off that little white patch on his chest. "I didn't break in. I simply used magic to gain entry," he explained in a languid drawl. "And it's six in the morning, a perfectly good time to wake up and share some breakfast with your new mentor."

I stared at Mr. Fluffikins, mouth agape. Not only had he shown up inside my bedroom at this unseemly hour, but now he expected me to make breakfast, too? Well, I hope he liked cold cereal, because that's all he was getting.

"Wait for me downstairs," I commanded, but Fluffikins did not budge. "I mean it. I'm not wearing any pants and need some time to make myself decent."

"You didn't seem too concerned about appearing decent last night," he bit out.

Oh, no. I was not about to be slut-shamed by a talking cat. "Get out of here!" I screamed and threw my pillow at him.

At least this time he listened. "The others will be

here soon, so please do make haste," he informed me on his way out.

"Oh, I'll make something, all right," I muttered under my breath as I hurried to pull on the first pants I found.

When I emerged from my room, I was wearing pajama bottoms and a tank top. I refused to make myself any less comfortable when Fluffikins would likely disapprove of whatever I wore anyway.

He sat waiting at my kitchen table—or rather, on it. He'd been joined by a stern-looking woman I recognized from the boardroom yesterday, although she hadn't spoken much then and didn't make very much of an impression now.

"Tawny," Fluffikins rasped. "This is Greta. She'll be helping with your orientation today."

"Hi, Greta," I said as I passed them both and made my way to the fridge. I didn't keep much food on hand, but I had an entire shelf full of my favorite cold brew coffees. I grabbed one, twisted off the cap, and took a long, life-giving gulp. Definitely the best part of my morning, especially since my shower was still on the fritz.

When I lowered the glass bottle, I found both of my uninvited guests staring openly at me.

"Greta is our school liaison for the region," the

cat said. "She looks after our interests as far as public education is concerned, much like how Barnes watches the police force."

I nodded. "Got it."

Hmmm, why did Greta get to go by her first name while Fluffikins always called Parker by his last?

Instead of answering my unspoken question, my new boss said, "As I'm sure you've already determined for yourself, she's the perfect person to begin your magical education."

Greta drummed her fingers on the tabletop and offered me a smile. "Shall we begin?"

"First, breakfast," Fluffikins corrected, then actually had the audacity to lick his chops. "I'm afraid I didn't have time to grab any for myself before coming here."

You could have come later, I thought. *Much later.*

"Breakfast, fine. What do magical cats like to eat?"

Fluffikins and Greta exchanged an amused glance.

"All cats are magical," she told me with a chuckle. "It's only people that aren't."

I ignored the implication that I should have already known the ins and outs of their strange secret world and got right back to the point. "So, what? You want some canned tuna or something?"

"Hey! That stereotype is offensive," the black cat hissed. "I'd much more prefer a fine cut of steak."

"I don't have any steak." And even if I did, I wouldn't be up to preparing it for a bossy cat first thing in the morning, especially since I only ever bought enough for one—me. "I don't even think I have tuna, come to mention it. How about a bowl of milk?"

He sighed and laid down on his side, shedding his fine black hairs all over my formerly clean kitchen table. "I suppose it will have to do, although I'll have you know, I'm lactose intolerant. Then again, I do deserve a bit of a treat with—" he looked me up and down "—all the stress I've been under lately. Next time, however, I expect you to be better prepared."

Apparently Fluffikins had never heard the whole thing about beggars and how they can't also be choosers. He was super lucky this was a job I couldn't quit and that the magic was enough of a draw to get me to swallow my pride and pour the last of my skim milk into a bowl for him.

I took my morning cereal dry.

What a way to start to the day!

*a*fter a very quick yet somehow also very uncomfortable breakfast, Fluffikins excused himself, leaving me and Greta to ourselves.

"So you want to learn how to be a Town Witch?" she asked, quirking an eyebrow made of such light hair that it almost looked translucent. Something was off about Greta, but I couldn't figure out what.

Realizing I had started to stare, I forced my gaze toward the floor. "Not that I want to, per se, more like I've been instructed to."

She laughed at this, and it sounded like the tinkling of bells. "Ah, the good old PTA. Nobody applies and yet everyone gets a job."

My stomach churned at the acronym. I'd been burned by the PTA before, and even though these three letters represented an entirely different organization this time, a fresh wave of outrage still washed over me.

Greta studied me in such a way that made me wonder if her powers came with the ability to read minds. I was just about to ask when she cleared her throat and said, "Let's start at the beginning. Shall we? Do you know what a Town Witch does?"

I shook my head. "All I know is that the magic is tied to the town, and that Lila Haberdash had the job until somebody snuck into her house and killed her."

Greta cringed. Her pale skin turned pink, making her whitish-blonde hair even more pronounced. "Yes, both those things are true."

"Wait. Has it officially been ruled a murder now?" I'd been so caught up in the magic stuff that I'd done a poor job following up on the investigative side of the situation.

"Oh, yes, but we knew that right away," she answered with a flippant wave. "Magic inevitably comes to an abrupt and violent end. *Always.*"

My stomach catapulted at that, threatening to spew the delicious coffee I'd only just entrusted to it. "How?"

Greta cocked her head to the side. "How what? How did she die? Magic, obviously."

"Oh." Well, that was clear as mud. I still didn't know an awful lot about magic, but if Fluffikins was looking for evidence that I hadn't done the deed, then the means should definitely be proof enough of my innocence.

"Try not to worry about it, dear," Greta said with a pinched expression as she grabbed my hand and gave it a squeeze. "Lila lived a good life while she still had it. For now, it's your turn to take up the Beech Grove Witch mantle, and soon it will be someone else's."

"The killer's, you mean?"

She sighed and let go of my hand. "That's often how these things work, yes."

I had at least a million questions but sensed her patience with me was already wearing thin. "Okay, so what do I need to know in order to do this job?"

And to not get killed, while I'm at it.

Greta gave me the first genuine grin I'd seen since meeting her. It brightened her whole face, which, when combined with her pale blond hair, gave her an almost angelic appearance.

"Let me escort you to your new office, and I'll explain some things along the way." She crossed my living room like she owned the place and held the door open so I could exit in front of her.

Even before we stepped foot off the porch, I knew we were headed to Mrs. Haberdash's main residence. My new office was the crime scene. *Wonderful.*

"The Town Witch," Greta explained as she fell into step beside me with a smooth, even stride, "acts as a conduit for the magic that occurs naturally within the land this town was built upon. So she has her own magic but can also pull from the stores of magic that belong to the town."

I bobbed my head as if this all made perfect sense. In theory, it did. But in practice? Well, that was another matter entirely.

"Why would she need to use the land's magic?" I asked.

"To protect the town and all its residents. As you can probably guess, it's a very important job." She quickened her pace, and I had to jog to keep up. Was this to prevent me from asking any more questions? Because it only gave me more—like why would she need to be evasive with me?

Instead I asked, "So if this is such an important job, why would you choose to entrust it to me? I didn't even know magic existed until less than twenty-four hours ago."

"Oh, it wasn't my choice, dear." She snorted in a rather unladylike way that clashed with the grace with which she carried herself. "It wasn't anyone's choice. You simply happened to be at the right place at the right time."

"Or the wrong one," I couldn't help muttering aloud.

She stopped and turned back to study me again, as if searching for something she'd tried and failed to find before.

"You won't have to do much," Greta reasoned after a couple uncomfortable moments of silence. "In fact, you won't be able to."

"Because the killer already got away with all of the town's magic," I filled in.

"Yes, but he or she will be back. And soon."

Finally I caught up with her and asked, "Why's that?"

She let out a shaky breath. "Because if the magic is kept away from its source for too long, it will die—and its vessel will die right along with it."

I shivered in the cool morning air. Well, at least the stakes weren't high or anything...

13

*G*reta and I finished our trek to Mrs. Haberdash's main house without saying anything else. Suddenly the desire to understand this new world of magic paled in comparison to the knowledge that the killer would be returning to the scene of the crime and I'd be right there waiting.

The house sat dark and empty, as if a part of it had died along with its owner.

"I'm glad it's just us this time," I said, remembering the strange run-in I'd had with the young woman yesterday. I glanced toward the tall aged tree where her floppy sunhat had gotten stuck and was surprised to find it gone.

The girl had most definitely left without it,

which meant she'd also come back. Probably in the dead of night.

"What do you mean? Who else were you expecting to find?" Greta asked, watching me closely. Always watching.

"Oh, I just meant Parker," I said, preferring to keep at least some of my cards close to the chest.

Greta shook her head. "He's already got more than enough to handle in his role as liaison to the force. Notice how there isn't any crime scene tape around? Lila was one of ours. Getting the normie police involved would only slow down the inevitable."

"The return of the killer, you mean?"

Greta's expression blanked. "What? Oh, yes. Of course, that's what I meant."

Uh-huh. I was starting to realize I couldn't even trust Greta as far as I could throw her, which wasn't far at all, given my disdain for regular exercise. Still, she was who I had right now. I'd learn whatever I could from her and then check back with Parker— or, heck, even Fluffikins—for confirmation later.

Greta smiled over at me, but I could tell it wasn't genuine. "There's no time like the present. Let's get down to business." She swept her hand in an upward flourish and the front door creaked open.

The first thing I noticed was that Mrs. Haber-dash's body had been cleared away. The grand entryway sat empty, but something in the air shimmered almost like a mirage. It was as if the house itself were waiting for something. Was that something me?

I stepped inside and felt its energy envelop me like a warm bath. Granted, I much preferred hot showers, but this new sensation relaxed me all the same. In fact, it almost felt as if I were floating. That was silly, of course, given that I was standing firmly on the hardwood floor. Nothing looked different. It's just that *I felt* different.

Greta walked a slow circle around me, muttering to herself. Her whispered words were too quiet for me to make out, not until she stopped in front of me and grabbed onto both of my wrists, holding them at the pulse points. "It's calling to you. Isn't it?"

I nodded. What was the point in arguing?

"Then the first part was much easier than we expected it to be. The town has already accepted you as a host for its magic."

"But this is supposed to be temporary," I argued, unable to tear my eyes away from her intent, blistering gaze.

"That was the initial plan, yes, but we have to listen to what the land wants, too."

"Which is me?" I squeaked.

"It most certainly seems that way."

"But its magic is with Mrs. Haberdash's murderer," I pointed out without blinking, afraid to look away. I didn't like where this was headed. It was even worse than the mind control Fluffikins and Parker had both exerted over me. I could avoid a single person, but what if the land itself decided it wanted to influence me? My only hope would be to move away from town—which, sure, I didn't have roots down or anything, but it would still take time to make a run for it.

"For now. There are ways to change that, of course."

"You don't mean—"

"That you kill the killer and claim the magic for yourself?" she asked with a smirk.

I gulped hard and nodded. Did she honestly expect me to take a life as part of a stupid temp job? Magic was cool and all, but not cool enough to make me change the core of my beliefs. Murder was wrong. That should have been a given here.

Greta crossed her arms over her chest and

shifted her weight from one side to the other. "Of course that's what I mean."

"I'm not killing anybody," I argued fruitlessly. For all I knew, Greta or any of the others could force me to do it with their mind control magic.

"We'll see," my supposed mentor told me with a light laugh.

My stomach dropped to the floor right beside where Mrs. Haberdash's body had lain sprawled less than twenty-four hours ago.

I liked the idea of magic, but in practice, it was proving to be way too much for me to handle. I wasn't a witch, but I was even less of a murderer.

Whether or not the intended victim was guilty of a terrible crime, it definitely wasn't my job to mete out justice.

But just how easily could I quit the Paranormal Temp Agency and resume my normal life as if nothing had ever happened?

I was beginning to feel this situation had escalated to *do or die.*

What would happen if I refused both those options?

14

Greta showed me around the house, which frankly appeared to be falling apart at the seams. She walked me through each room, describing the items in it and what purpose each held. It was boring with a capital *B*.

Seriously, how was any of this meant to contribute to my magical training? We were already working on a tight schedule here, and instead of teaching me spells or potions, my assigned mentor spent the last ten minutes describing how Mrs. Haberdash had bespelled her socks to make them three degrees warmer than room temperature. Not even the magic she'd used to accomplish the task, mind you—just the fact she'd done it at all.

How was any of this supposed to help me catch a

killer? Every single time I tried to ask a more rele-
vant question, Greta brushed me off by changing the
topic. At this rate, I might learn to tailor my pants
with magic by the time the day was through, but I'd
never learn anything cooler like how to fly or... I
don't know, evade a death blow, maybe.

The only thing that managed to keep my attention at all was the bedroom closet. Greta drifted in
and began flipping through the previous tenant's
wardrobe, explaining the type of Town Witch duties
each selection could be worn for.

Ugh. Why did I need to know any of this?

My mind wandered yet again, turning Greta's
nasally voice into a buzzing drone as I glanced
around the room in search of something more interesting to ponder over. That's when the fantastic
black hat sitting on the top shelf of that closet caught
my eye.

Of course, I had no qualms about interrupting
Greta, seeing as I hadn't really been listening
anyway. "What's that?" I asked, motioning toward
the black velvet hat that had been embellished with
a purple satin sash.

Greta's eyes lit when they landed upon it. "Oh,
good find. This is the most important item in a Town
Witch's entire wardrobe and possibly the single most

important item she owns. I can't believe the murderer would have left this here."

Instead of waiting for her to explain further, I grabbed the hat off the shelf and unfurled the top, finding it ended in a perfect delightful point.

A burst of energy shot straight into my chest, lighting me from the inside. The hat was speaking to me in the only way it could—through its magic. Without so much as a second thought, I plopped it right on top of my newly pinkened hair. And the exact moment that witch's hat hit my head, a vivid picture filled my mind. I saw Mrs. Haberdash going about her business, checking the mail (proof she'd received my letters!), heading to the kitchen to make tea, and then...

She dropped the kettle to the floor with a crash that sent hot water flying everywhere. I couldn't just see and hear it, I felt the burn, too. I glanced down but only saw my own feet beneath me.

"It's time then?" Mrs. Haberdash asked with a gasp while my vision had been pulled away.

I closed my eyes to snap my attention back to the scene unfolding in my mind, but all I saw was the spilled water on the floor.

A heavy weight settled on my chest, turning breathing into a struggle. The sound of echoing footsteps approached, but I couldn't see who was there with her—with me.

A rush of wind blew over me and an icy chill wrapped itself around me. The scene snapped out of focus and...

"What are you doing?" Greta cried, holding the hat clutched firmly in one manicured hand as she stared at me in horror.

"The hat," I murmured, still trying to make sense of what had just happened. "I think it wanted to show me what happened to Mrs. Haberdash."

"I told Fluffikins this was a bad idea," she spat as she shoved the hat back into the closet. After she slammed the doors shut, she formed a *C* with her thumb and index finger and moved them in a swift pendulum motion.

"We have to find out what happened. Mrs. Haberdash deserves justice." I ran toward the closet and pulled hard at it, but the doors wouldn't budge.

"That's not your job," Greta snapped.

"But I'm the new Town Witch for—"

"You're a temp!" she exploded, leaving me behind as she charged out of the room. "And I refuse to train someone with so little regard for..."

I chased her from the room, down the hall, and

to the top of stairs. Greta now stood stock-still, not moving or speaking, hardly even breathing.

"What's happening?" I asked in a desperate whisper. "Why aren't you—?"

But then my legs locked in place, frozen. In fact, the only part of me I could still move was my eyes. I directed my gaze to the base of the stairs, and that's when I saw her.

The same young woman I'd met the day before stood at the ground level with both arms raised.

"You again," she said with a cold smile. "You should have stayed out of this while you had the chance."

She was definitely right about that.

I wanted to look to Greta for guidance, but I could barely make her out in my peripheral vision. I hoped she had a plan, because I sure didn't.

15

I twisted and wriggled, but still I couldn't escape the young witch's magical grip. I was straining hard enough to break out into a sweat, but my limbs didn't so much as twitch from all that effort. She had me in a powerful hold, and I didn't have the slightest hope of defending myself if this encounter turned violent.

"Melony Haberdash," Greta growled between clenched teeth, remaining perfectly still as she stared the other woman down. "I should have guessed it would be you."

Melony's cruel stare softened, but her grip held tight. "Just so you know, I had nothing to do with my great aunt's murder. Why would I kill her when I was next in line to inherit her position?"

She paused briefly, then her eyes snapped to me with a burning new intensity. "I found this one stalking around the property yesterday, and now she's here again today. Doesn't seem like such a coincidence. Does it?"

Great's voice came out choked. "No, you've got it wrong. She's just the temp."

"Ha! Seems to me like you're playing right into her hand. First she steals the magic and then she gets free training from the board by playing innocent. That's pretty brilliant, actually. Maybe I should be taking notes."

Greta continued to struggle beside me. A flash of movement below her hip suggested she'd regained control of her fingers but still couldn't move her full hand yet. "She's a normie, I swear to you. At first I had my suspicions, too, but she honestly knows nothing. She just almost killed herself by replaying the murder."

My heart practically stopped at this new revelation. *I'd almost died?* Just by putting on that witch's hat? *Yikes.* That meant Greta had saved me from my foible. At first I'd thought she'd cut the encounter short because she didn't want me to discover that she was the killer, but now it seemed like she'd chosen to protect me. Is that why she was wasting time rather than giving me any real training?

Whatever her reasons for keeping me naive, I sure could use some magical ability right now.

All I had were the instincts Fluffikins had high-lighted last night, but Melony had set a trap that caught us off guard. Neither Greta nor I had a chance to react before falling under her spell.

That left the one thing I'd always had, even before I knew about magic. *My words.*

It was time to speak up for myself. If I could convince Melony I wasn't a threat, maybe she would let me go.

"I didn't kill Mrs. Haberdash," I shouted at her through tears. "I've never killed anyone. I shouldn't even be here. This is clearly business that I have no part of. I never asked to be made a witch. I just write books!"

Melony studied me, sizing me up the same way Greta had earlier. She must have found what she was looking for because a few seconds later the magical vise snapped open and I fell to the ground.

"Where's my aunt's hat?" the young witch asked me as I picked myself up.

I turned back toward the room we'd just exited. "I'll go get it for—"

"No!" Greta screamed, but it was too late. Melony was already charging up the stairs and into her late aunt's bedroom.

"What have you done?" Greta muttered, still bound tightly by Melony's magic.

"But she said she didn't..." My words fell away. Why had I believed her when she clearly had the most to gain from Mrs. Haberdash's untimely demise?

"She's not the killer," Greta admitted as she turned her head very slightly to look toward me. Little by little, the spell was thawing, but would Greta be free in enough time to stop Melony from getting away?

She grunted from the strain of trying to break the spell, then added, "I could tell she was speaking the truth with us just now, but—"

"Yes!" Melony cried from the other room, causing Greta to stop mid-sentence. "I've got you now."

"Hey! What did you see? Do you know who did it?" I asked as she rushed back down the stairs, cradling the old hat against her chest, without so much as a second glance toward me and Greta. Maybe I should have continued to play dumb, but if she'd spoken truthfully before, perhaps she would do so now. My gift of verbal persuasion was the only option I had, since I didn't know how to summon my new magic on command.

But Melony ignored us both, flinging open the front door and charging outside. As soon as the door slammed behind her, the hold on Greta released completely.

She fell to the floor, weak and heaving.

"What happened?" I asked as I helped her back onto her feet.

Greta's eyes appeared vacant as she explained, "She used the hat to call up the murder scene just like you did, but as a more experienced witch she knows how to manipulate the memories so they don't pose a threat to her."

"She saw the murderer," I said with a sharp inhale.

Greta nodded meekly. "Yes. And she's on her way to kill him to assume the town magic."

I'd done this. I'd found the hat and then I'd guided Melony straight to it. I still didn't know who'd killed Mrs. Haberdash, but it would be my fault when that person met their untimely end. And it would be my fault when the crazed teenager was filled with some of the strongest magic in the region, which I doubted she'd use to make things better for its residents.

Gulp.

16

Two choices. That's what I had at this point.

I could buckle down to help Greta, Parker, Fluffikins, and crew find—and save—the murderer. But once we saved him or her, did they want me to do the killing for them?

I was still so confused about what was expected of me here. Magic was weird, and yet the rules that governed it were weirder still. It also seemed like they shifted according to who I was talking to at the moment. If Greta wanted me to stay on permanently, what did Fluffikins think? Or Parker? Did they expect me to kill for them? If I remained steadfast in my refusal, would they force me to comply?

This brought me to option number two. I could get the heck out of here and pretend this whole thing had never happened.

"Okay, so good luck with everything!" I shouted to Greta before I sprinted down the stairs just as fast as my feet would carry me.

What? I hadn't survived thirty-five years on this earth by having no sense of self-preservation. All the other players here had magic. *Real magic!*

Yeah, they'd given me a temporary dose, but I definitely didn't know enough to protect myself. Besides, Melony was already on her way to off the killer and assume her aunt's stolen magic. They didn't need me as a temp anymore, and they definitely didn't need me as a contract killer. Way too much could go wrong there, and I refused to jeopardize my entire life and future.

Now if I didn't help them, which I wasn't going to, my life would still be pretty up in the air. No matter what happened, I'd be living in the backyard of a murderer—Melony.

That would be bad. *Hmmm.*

I ran through my options a couple more times while racing back to the guest cottage I called home. Despite everything, at least my running shoes were finally living up to their name.

By the time I reached the front door, I'd made up my mind all over again. It was time to check the real estate listings online and move myself as far from this crazy place as I could. Honestly, the sooner the better. I'd just fire up my laptop and...

And nothing, at least not yet.

It seemed I had a guest.

"I heard trouble is brewing," Mr. Fluffikins announced from his perch on the back of my sofa, one paw crossed daintily over the other.

I eyed him suspiciously. "Yeah, it just started like five minutes ago. How did you get here so fast? Did you teleport or something?"

He hung his head and laughed. "Of course not. *I flew.*"

"Oh, yes, because that makes more sense."

The black cat remained seated, watching me closely.

I sighed, knowing if I didn't say something soon, he'd start making all sorts of demands. I still didn't want this stupid temp job, and I wasn't exactly up to playing the kindly hostess, either.

"Why are you here?" I said with a scowl. "You don't need me anymore."

Fluffikins stood and stretched, arching his back high like a cat on Halloween or a seriously talented yogi, or both. "Actually, we need you more than ever. Come with me."

"I'm sorry, this is all a little much for me. I'd really rather not die today. Or any day, really. But especially not today. Thanks."

"Then it's imperative you stay under my protection, and I can't look after you if you're running away. Now can I?"

Crud. He had a point.

I rolled my shoulders, but the nervous tension remained. "Why am I a part of this? Why do you need me at all?"

"You might want to be sitting for this," Fluffikins said slowly, almost compassionately.

I sunk down onto the sofa, and Fluffikins came over to situate himself on my lap.

"Now pet me," he ordered, locking me in his glowing golden gaze. I knew petting an animal was supposed to be good for your blood pressure, but I needed a lot more than that to calm me down.

So I refused. "I'm good, thanks."

"Pet me!" he commanded in a way that brooked no argument.

He didn't force me with his powers, but I still complied, finding it easier to get through whatever he wanted so I could carry on with my normal life—boring but happy, just what I needed.

The moment my fingers made contact with his silky black hair, a new vision flooded my brain. It was like what I'd experienced with the hat, but even more vivid, possibly because it was being projected by a living being instead of an inanimate object.

Fluffikins purred softly but otherwise didn't interrupt as I explored his memories.

With a hitched breath, I yanked my hand back, cutting the vision short. I'd already seen more than enough. Much to my surprise, Fluffikins had revealed an answer I didn't expect but also couldn't contest after having witnessed it so clearly.

"You did it," I choked out, sliding him off my lap and hopping back to my feet. "You ordered the hit on Mrs. Haberdash."

But why was he telling me now? And why hadn't he told me before? Was this some kind of Bond villain moment where he revealed the beauty of his plan before offing the victim?

And where did I actually fit into all of this?

Was it just dumb luck, or was something greater at play here?

I didn't want to know, but I needed to find out.

Knowledge was power, and it might have been the only thing that could save me now.

17

I pointed a shaky finger at Fluffikins, who was still seated on the sofa in front of me. "You killed my landlady. She was your... your colleague, if not your friend. Why should I listen to anything you have to say? And why should I help you?"

"I didn't kill her," the cat said in that strange breathless way of his, not so much as lifting paw as he regarded me calmly.

I, however, continued to shout. "But you hired the killer. That makes you just as good as."

He stood and stretched. "I don't have time to debate this with you, Tawny, so I'll cut straight to the point. Do you want more people to die or not?"

Honestly, I just wanted this to all go away, but

despite all the magic involved in this horrible situation, that didn't seem to be an option. "I still don't know why I'm a part of this. Can't you just go away and leave me alone?"

"We never meant to involve anyone outside of the board," he admitted with a sad shake of his head. "But when you stumbled upon Lila's body, we had no choice but to bring you in."

"You knew I didn't kill her. This whole time, you knew!" I sputtered. "And since you're the one who ordered the hit, I'm willing to bet you know who the real killer is, too. So, why make me a temp? Why give me magic at all?"

"We took you in for your protection. The rest of it was a ruse, to misdirect anyone who showed up to sniff around Lila's murder with the hopes of gaining her magic. And, look, that's precisely what happened. You would have been a target, no matter what, having shown up yesterday morning."

"You made me a target!" This was the one point I just couldn't get past. Even though I'd accidentally walked onto the scene, there had to be countless other ways to keep me safe. Giving me magic seemed mighty extreme, especially since they hadn't done much to teach me to use it. What was the whole point?

"You were already a target," Fluffikins shouted back, losing his calm for the first time since the conversation had started. "Playing into it bought us all time, but now that time has run out. We can't stand here arguing. We need to act while we still have time!"

"I don't understand. If Melony isn't coming for you or for me, then who is she after?"

"She's going after the actual killer, the person who absorbed the town magic. She wants it for herself by any means possible. We need to get to him before Melony does."

"To who?" I demanded, stomping my foot. The more Fluffikins explained, the less I understood. "Who are we rushing off to save now?"

"The person who killed Lila Haberdash. Barnes."

My mind kind of exploded then. Fluffikins had ordered Parker to kill Mrs. Haberdash? I really wanted to know the why, but I also believed Fluffikins when he said our time was running out.

I still had to ask. "Parker killed her? Why? Why would he do that?" My voice trembled as I tested these words aloud.

"Because it's what Lila wanted," he admitted. His chest heaved with the weight of this revelation, making the little white patch bob within the mass of black fur.

I raised an eyebrow at him. I believed what he was telling me, but that didn't mean I understood. A part of me doubted I'd ever fully understand, no matter how many questions I asked. "She wanted someone to murder her?"

"Yes, and she trusted us to get it done right." He hopped off the couch and landed by my feet.

"None of this makes any sense!"

Fluffikins stared up at me with bright golden eyes that seemed to see right through me. "Can you please just trust me on this? We've lost too much time already. Do you want to save Barnes or not?"

I'd seen the look in Melony's eyes as she first questioned Greta and me and then charged out of the house with that enchanted hat. She was out for blood. *Parker's blood.*

And I also knew deep in my gut that Parker was an okay guy. He'd been kind to me and seemed earnest in wanting to help me. Even if he'd been the one to get me mixed up in this whole magical business—which I still did not appreciate, by the way—it didn't mean he deserved to die for it.

"But how can I help? I'm just a human," I mumbled, feeling so useless in that moment.

Fluffikins's eyes twinkled. "Ah, but you have magic now. What do you say? Join the good guys?"

Well, what choice did I have now? The stakes felt much higher now that someone I knew and liked was in jeopardy. I sighed and nodded. "If you're sure you need me and that you'll keep me safe, then I'm in."

"Great. We've already wasted more time than I'd prefer, but luckily Melony is a low level witch. She'll have needed to travel by the traditional means, so we still have time to beat her to our destination. Follow me." The cat ran to the door and let himself outside.

I followed after, wondering if I was crazy for agreeing to help with what little information I'd been given.

"Now grab my tail," Fluffikins shouted into the still morning sky.

I crouched down, closed my eyes, and clenched that tail like my life depended on it. The soft fluffy appendage turned hard in my grip and then it started to grow. When I opened my eyes again, I was no longer holding onto a tail but rather a broomstick, and I was no longer standing in my front yard.

I was flying.

18

The speeding wind whipped the bottoms of my pajama pants against my ankles—or rather it was the speeding me on top of the broom that I'd somehow managed to conjure from my talking feline escort's tail.

Fluffikins flew effortlessly at my side. He looked as if he were suspended mid-leap as he zipped through the air like a bullet.

So there we were, racing against time to save a killer from being killed, because apparently he'd killed for the right reasons while his would-be killer wanted to kill him for the wrong reasons.

Yeah, I was confused, too.

I was also more than a little upset that I'd ended up wearing my frumpy PJs for this momentous encounter. I didn't have much time to worry about either of these things, though, because Fluffikins and I arrived at our destination a couple short minutes after we'd departed.

I recognized the office complex from my visits the day before. This seemed like a good place to start, but would Parker even be there? He'd told me he had a regular policeman's job, too, which meant he probably didn't spend all day waiting around Paranormal HQ just in case the boss cat needed him.

Heck, for all I knew, Melony might have found him already.

Mr. Fluffikins muttered something under his breath, and the glass-topped conference room opened up like a blossoming flower. Pink glittering magic swirled about us as the building sucked us in like a Venus flytrap.

My broom disappeared and I lurched toward the floor. But then the pink stuff caught me and guided me gently into one of the many executive chairs that lined the table. This felt similar to the sensation I'd experienced in Mrs. Haberdash's house, like I was floating in a bath of perfectly temperate water. The pink pulsed gently, calming and comforting me, providing a featherlight massage.

Fluffikins landed in front of me in a perfectly

graceful and well executed maneuver that was all his own. The pink magic parted to allow him passage rather than coaxing him forward like it had done for me.

"I hereby call an emergency board meeting," he said, his words echoing around the room. "All liaisons are required."

The pink magic gathered into a ball and bounced up through the open roof into the sky above.

"Wh-what's going on? Where's P-Parker?" I sputtered. I felt the absence of the atmospheric magic acutely despite having only been under its effects for a few seconds.

Fluffikins paced the length of the table anxiously. "He's on his way, along with the others. I rarely call an emergency meeting, but when I do, they have no choice but to travel here immediately."

"What's all this pink glittery stuff?" I asked, watching as it twisted and danced just above the open ceiling. "I didn't see it when I was here yesterday."

"You didn't have magic when you were in the board room yesterday. It was here, but you couldn't yet see it. It's always here," he answered distractedly as he continued to cross the table back and forth.

"What is it?" I wanted to know, but more than that I needed to keep him talking, to protect me from my own thoughts and worries.

"It's but a small piece of the earth's most concentrated and most powerful magic, taken right from its very core. Each of our agencies around the globe has been granted a part to keep us connected to the whole. It works to stabilize the balance within each region and prevent any one center from gaining too much power." He spoke so smoothly and eloquently that I wondered if he was quoting something or someone verbatim.

"How does it do that?"

Pace, pace, pace.

I was growing more frightened by the minute, especially since Fluffikins appeared rattled, too.

He took a few more loops of the table and then plopped himself down across from me. "By sparking non-magical humans' so-called intuition and influencing them to act in a way that is good for humanity as a whole, even if they believe they are acting on selfish desires."

"Huh. I've got to admit, this is all a bit out there. I was just coming around to this whole Town Witch thing, and now you expect me to wrap my head around a living strain of magic that balances all of humanity?"

He shrugged. "You asked. I merely answered."

"Why am I here?"

"Because the magic chose you. There was a reason you discovered Lila's body, that you bumped into Barnes, even that you were there when Melony showed up to reclaim the hat."

"I'm nobody special."

He nodded. "My inclination would be to agree with you, but the magic is always right."

I folded my arms across my chest. "If the magic is so high and mighty, then how come terrible things still happen every day? People are murdered, as we well know. Kids are taken from their parents, wars kill millions. Why doesn't the magic stop any of that from happening?"

"Balance encompasses both dark and light, good and bad. It's difficult to understand for the uninitiated. Still, it has chosen you as someone who will play a significant role in what is to come."

"Now there are prophecies?" I gasped as goosebumps rose to my arms.

The cat's eyes flashed, but he quickly looked away, focusing his gaze just over my left shoulder.

"No, no. I have no idea what happens next, but whatever it is, you'll be an important player."

I bit my lip as I thought about this. Part of me wanted to yell at Fluffikins for dragging me deep into this agency mess without explaining any of it in a way I could actually understand, but another very big part of me understood that I'd have never agreed to get mixed up in things here if he'd led with any of the craziness that had come to light over the last few minutes.

"What if I'm not enough?" I asked instead. This wasn't just my greatest worry now. It was my greatest fear in life. I hadn't been enough for my ex-husband. My rate of producing books was quickly not becoming enough for my literary agent. With all those failures to my name, could I be enough for something that mattered this much?

Fluffikins fixed his eyes on me, unblinking. "Oh, but Tawny. You already are."

19

*N*ot even two minutes after Fluffikins's summons, the other members of the board began descending upon the room to join us at the table.

First came Greta. "I put the best wards on the house that I could to bolster the ones already there. Lila's spells are fading fast now that she's no longer in residence," she informed us before she'd even landed in her spot.

Next came the old guy in the suit. "You've removed me from a very important procession, I'll have you know."

"It will wait," his cat boss snarled. "What we have now affects the entire region across all departments."

The old guy blinked hard and his mouth hung slightly agape. "All?"

Fluffikins nodded solemnly as two more liaisons fell from the sky and took their rightful seats. "Now let's begin."

"Wait? Where's Parker?" I choked out as I searched the sky for his familiar form. "Why isn't he here yet?"

"If he is able, then he will come," Greta said from the seat beside me, reaching under the table to squeeze my hand.

If? But hadn't Fluffikins said attendance was required? Did Greta mean he might already be dead or incapacitated?

I clung tight to her hand, needing whatever small comfort I could find there.

"Beginning now." Fluffikins began to pace up and down the table once again. This time like a general. "First let me say, I'm sorry to have acted without the full board's knowledge, especially now that I see my quick action did not have a positive effect on the outcome."

He paused, but nobody spoke to fill the silence. We all waited.

"Lila Haberdash was compromised," the cat revealed. "And so she requested that I organize her death so that we could control the passage of the town's magic to its next host."

Gasps rose up around the room. Only Greta beside me did not react. She already knew, I realized then. She knew everything, all of it. And she clearly disagreed, at least with my involvement in the fallout. Not because she didn't like me, but because she wanted to protect me. My first impression of her had been completely wrong.

"How was she compromised?" the old guy asked.

Fluffikins stopped and raised a paw to his forehead as if in pain. "Lila's grandniece, Melony Haberdash, manipulated her grandfather into revealing the family's magical legacy, including how power was passed from one heir to the next."

"So she was going to kill Mrs. Haberdash," I supplied.

"Yes, Lila certainly thought so. Magic isn't meant to be revealed until the preparations for a transfer are nearly complete, precisely to prevent this kind of thing from happening. But Lila's brother, Melony's grandfather, always resented that the magic had skipped him as the first born and gone to his sister. My guess is Melony didn't have to press too hard to gain the information she sought."

"I warned you," the old guy said with a sad shake

of his head. "Lila was a great asset to this town, but she didn't come from good stock. That brother of hers never recovered from losing out on the position, even though he wasn't even suited to it in the first place. Now he's sending his heirs two generations down to cause trouble? We should have taken him out years ago when he first started causing trouble."

"Lila never wanted harm to come to her family. I think a small part of her always hoped they could reconcile," Greta answered. "It was only right to respect her wishes."

"Lila was one of the good ones," Fluffikins agreed. "Unfortunately, her family took advantage of her kind heart."

"What's Melony going to do now? And how do we know she's acting alone? If her grandfather started this, couldn't he still be in on it?" I asked aloud. On the inside I still yearned for Parker. What if Melony had already gotten to him? What if I never saw him again?

"We don't know what the plan is, only that it needs to be stopped," Greta explained softly, still holding tight to my hand.

"Well, where is she? Can't we lock her up in a magical prison and throw away the key? We've got to do something!"

"It's not that simple," the cat argued.

"Magic always comes to a violent end," Greta said, echoing the same warning she'd given me earlier.

"Then why would you put Parker at risk like this? If you knew Melony was coming for Lila, shouldn't you have all known that she would come for him when she realized what had happened?" A mass of rage began to form in my gut. They'd knowingly endangered Parker. It wasn't right.

Fluffikins sighed. "We didn't have as much time as we'd hoped. Ultimately, Barnes volunteered to pick up the mantle because he didn't want to risk Greta in his place."

She squeezed my hand under the table. "He said the worst thing that could happen would be to compromise our schools. If we want a better world, then we need to guard the future like the treasure it is."

No wonder I liked the guy. He was handsome, brave, and loved kids. If I wasn't such a pessimist about love, I may have succumbed to the crush that was threatening to overtake my heart. Instead I swallowed down all the many things I was feeling in that moment and asked the one thing that mattered most. "How do we stop Melony?"

I decided then and there that I would help in whatever way I could. Whether it was to protect Parker or to avenge him, I was fully in.

20

*D*espite the urgency of my question and the fact that it was a pretty great one to ask, Fluffikins failed to acknowledge it.

Perhaps he would have, but one of the liaisons immediately hopped to her feet and placed a hand on each of her ample hips. "Why wasn't the entire board informed? I personally would have loved to hear about all this before it all hit the fan."

"Apologies, Connie," the cat drawled. Was he actually sucking up to her when he was the one in charge? "Lila preferred that as few people as possible know about the plan to preemptively end her life. As you know, it's the ultimate sacrifice and highest duty for a Town Witch to die protecting her town. She knew what needed to be done, and she didn't want anyone trying to change her mind."

"But *she* knew." Connie pointed at Greta accusingly. Her growled words sent a shiver right through me. They didn't exactly sound human, but what else could they be? "What does this decision even have to do with her department? Nothing, that's what!"

The cat's patience had now worn thin. He sighed and rubbed at his forehead with a paw. "You know very well, indeed, that as the liaison of Schools, Greta is the most equipped to handle situations that impact the future. Besides, Melony is young, still a student herself. At least once this summer is over, she is expected to head to the Academy and begin—"

"That's not happening now, obviously," Greta interjected with a sullen expression.

"And Parker was informed," Fluffikins continued as he directed an unhappy glare at Connie, "because the impending crime fell directly into his role as liaison to the Force."

"Still, Commerce would have liked to be notified," Connie pouted, refusing to back down.

"Agriculture, too," the plain-looking middle-aged man beside her chimed in. Excluding me and

Parker, he appeared to be the youngest in the group by at least two decades.

Everyone's eyes sought out the centenarian in the business suit.

"Nah," he said with a wave of his hand. "Cemetery is good. We prefer not to handle them until they need us to."

"Cemeteries?" I whispered to Greta.

"Yes, it's one of the five essential regional departments."

Now having heard a few new departments mentioned in rapid succession, I started a mental checklist. The PTA board had Police, Schools, Commerce, Agriculture, and Cemeteries—then there was the Town Witch and Fluffikins, of course. Whatever he did.

I decided to come right out and ask him. "Everybody here has a job, even me, although I'm just a temp. What's your role, Mr. Fluffikins?" I used the Mr. assuming he'd be more likely to answer my question if I showed him some respect in asking it.

"Why, I'm the Diplomat, of course. It is me who is in charge of this region as a whole." Well, I guessed that made sense. Little by little, I was starting to get it, but...

"I just have one question, though. Actually two. Wait, it's three."

He rolled his paw to signal for me to go ahead.

"Okay, so first, where's Parker? Also, how do we stop Melony? And if you have time, please explain why this place is called the Paranormal Temp Agency. It seems like nobody here is a temp except for me."

"Parker will be here as soon as he can if he can, and once we have him here, Melony will no doubt come to us. It's the best-case scenario since we have the global magic source to protect us."

I glanced up toward the ceiling where the glittering atmospheric magic had settled in like a heavy pink fog.

Fluffikins continued, "You're our only temp currently, but make no mistake, we have quite the revolving door of helpers."

"If that's the case, why not hire more people to your board on a full-time basis? Is it because you don't want to pay benefits?"

Across the table Connie chuckled, making her over-sized bosom bounce. I couldn't tell if she liked me or not, but I could definitely tell she wasn't a fan of Fluffikins.

The cat rolled his eyes before fixing them back

on me. "The magical balance is in constant flux, and thus our needs change. A majority of magic users keep their abilities discreet and go about to live a mostly normal human life."

"So it's only you guys who are supercharged?"

"We're the strongest," Greta said, "because we're able to use our abilities regularly. Practice makes perfect, after all." Now she finally sounded like a teacher. As I got to know everyone better, it was easier to understand how they fit into their roles.

"Okay, so let me see if I'm understanding this correctly," I said. "Most people don't have magic, and most of the people who *do* have magic don't really use it."

"Yes, other than instinctively as you saw during our orientation last night," the cat supplied.

Had that startling display of elemental wrath really only happened last night? Wow. It took me a second to process that before moving on.

"The liaisons are the strongest magic users because they use their powers regularly," I surmised.

"Yes, that's right," Greta encouraged.

"Okay, so then why are we all so afraid of this Melony chick? She's only—what?—eighteen?" I shuddered at the realization that I could practically be her mother. Thank goodness, I wasn't.

Everyone watched and waited for me to push forward with my train of thought, and so I did.

"She's not a liaison, which means she is not a regular magic practitioner. We know she has some, because of the confrontation Greta and I had with her, but—can someone please explain this next part —why is a room full of the region's most powerful magic folk hiding from a little girl?"

21

*N*obody spoke until at last Fluffikins took a deep breath and said, "That's not a bad question. We could easily overpower Melony, but just because we can doesn't mean we should."

I threw my hands up in the air—something I was doing a lot of lately, quite frankly. "Seriously, guys? One second you present yourselves as these noble defenders of the balance, and the next you talk yourselves out of easily solving a very simple problem. You do realize it's only going to turn into a much bigger problem, right? I mean, what happened to that whole noble balance spiel you just gave me like three minutes ago?"

Greta placed both hands flat on the table in front

of her. The whitish eyebrows framing bright blue eyes gave her an almost lupine appearance. "I understand there's much about our world you can't yet grasp, but there are nuances, which however small and seemingly inconsistent are important to uphold, especially for those in positions of power."

"So you're not dealing with Melony because —*what?*—it would look bad? Greta, you're the one who told me magic always comes to a violent end. Melony's the instigator here, so why aren't you taking action?" Whether or not I'd ended up with the PTA by some stupid fluke, I was here now and I would make my opinions known. Namely that their attempt at an explanation made little to no sense.

When Greta shook her head, one of her tight blonde curls fell out of place. "It's not our place to end a life."

"Are you kidding me?" I exploded. I couldn't help it. "You're the one who ended Mrs. Haberdash's!"

"At her request, yes. She made a sacrifice to protect this town, but also to protect her next of kin." Greta looked tired but not any less steadfast in her explanation. Even though their supposed logic wasn't making much sense to me, it clearly held up with her.

I softened my voice. Greta wasn't the enemy here. Flawed thinking aside, nobody in this room presented a threat to me or this town. Melony on the other hand... "Why would she want to save somebody who wanted to kill her? And what exactly do you plan to do when Melony shows up with the goal of offing Parker? And for the last time *where's Parker?* Because he certainly isn't here, and it seems plain old stupid to sit around waiting for whatever happens next when we can get out there and control the future!"

Fluffikins tsked. "Spoken like a true normie. Have you been listening to anything Greta or I have tried to explain?"

I turned all my frustration on the small black cat. "Yes, I'm listening, but all I hear is words and excuses. You have the power to end this, but instead you're sitting here helpless. You're not helpless, and you should be out there helping Parker!"

Fluffikins flexed his paws and the claws shout out menacingly. "I've never been so—"

"*Whoa, whoa, whoa.* Calm down." Parker's familiar voice floated down from above as he drifted toward his seat. "I'm right here."

The pink magic in the air shimmered briefly, then whooshed back to the ceiling. Now that everyone was accounted for, the glass ceiling closed in on itself, shutting out the larger world.

Greta placed a hand on my side and leaned toward me like she wanted to say something to me in private, but I didn't care to find out what that was.

Parker was here! He was okay!

I leaped out of my chair and ran over to hug him. It didn't matter that I hardly knew him—he was alive and quite possibly a hero. The fact that he'd been in uncertain danger made me realize just how much I instinctively liked him, right from the beginning.

He stood to meet me and winced as I wrapped both arms around him, but then settled into the embrace.

"Are you okay?" I whispered, pulling back to look into his eyes.

The sharp gray appeared dulled, but his smile appeared genuine. "I'm okay," he confirmed with a relieved sigh.

Fresh cuts and scrapes covered his face, neck, and arms, but none of them appeared too serious. What had held him back? Had he gone ahead and acted while the rest of the board sat here twiddling their thumbs?

I wouldn't put that past him.

Parker was one of them, but he was also different.

More human somehow.

Maybe it was because as a policeman, he was accustomed to seeing things in black and white—right or wrong. And what Melony wanted to do was wrong. Clearly, he saw that.

But despite these convictions, would he act against the boss cat's wishes? Had he already? I knew I was assuming a lot, but a part of me just knew Parker was one of the good guys. Maybe the best guy.

"I was so worried," I murmured, tightening my hold. I wanted him to be that hero, but even more than that I just wanted him to be safe and here with me. That crush I'd tried to prevent from taking hold had definitely wrapped its vise grip around my heart. *Stupid feelings.*

"Where were you?" Fluffikins demanded, stalking over to us. "Why the delay?"

Parker let me go. For a moment, he hung his head as if too tired to answer. But then he picked himself back up and said, "Melony came to see me."

Melony.

22

I put a hand on Parker's shoulder.

He flinched before glancing away. The smile that followed came a couple seconds too late to be natural.

Ugh. I was really worried about him now. Had something terrible already happened? Was he merely putting on a strong front for me and the others?

"What do you mean she came to see you?" I pressed, willing—*begging*—him to tell me the truth. "Are you sure you're okay?"

He pressed his lips in a straight line, then pulled out the chair in front of him and took a seat. "I'm here. Aren't I?"

"What happened?" I asked, refusing to leave his side even though it seemed I'd been dismissed.

"Enough, Tawny. Take your seat," Fluffikins commanded as he paced back to the head of the table, then plopped onto his rear. "Now. Give us the full report, Barnes."

I kept my eyes glued on Parker as I trudged back to my seat beside Greta.

Everyone waited with bated breath.

Parker folded his hands in front of him and sighed. "She caught up with me while I was on my way into the station. There were too many normies around, so I led her to an empty lot on the outskirts of town. I expected her to jump straight into an assault once we were both out of our cars, but instead she wanted to talk. Said the Town Witch job was hers, that it was bad enough her great aunt Lila had stolen it right out from under her grandfather, that she wasn't going to let the wrong person have the job for even a second longer."

"But you're here now, and you say you're okay," I said, dumbfounded. "So, what happened?"

"Tawny, silence!" Fluffikins bellowed and followed it up with a low, threatening growl. "I realize you have a lot of questions, but you are not the one who's in charge here."

Parker frowned. "She told me to surrender, but I refused. That was when she attacked. I tried not to hurt her, but she came at me so fast, I couldn't avoid..." His voice cracked, and he stopped speaking.

"We promised Lila she would remain unharmed," Greta interjected, popping to her feet so fast, her chair fell back behind her.

Parker ran his hands through his hair and let out a choked sob. "I know. I'm so sorry. It's the magic. With Lila's plus my own, it's too much. I couldn't control it."

"This is very worrying, indeed," Fluffikins said with a flick of his sleek black tail.

"I would have gotten here sooner, but I didn't want to lead Melony right to our HQ. That is, if she even managed to survive," Parker offered meekly. "I didn't know what else to do. I'm sorry if I've complicated matters for the board."

"So what happens now?" I asked when no one else moved to speak. "The threat is gone, right? So everything goes back to normal?"

"But at what cost?" Greta bit out, wrapping her arms around herself as she swayed on her feet. "You've defied Lila's last wish. Melony was the only remaining heir to the Haberdash legacy. Other than her grandfather, of course."

What was going on here? None of these explana-
tions were making things any clearer, so I asked a
question even though Fluffikins had ordered me to
stay silent. "So Melony would have become the
Town Witch eventually, anyway? If that's the case,
why would she kill her aunt? Just to make it happen
a little sooner?"

"She wasn't ready," Greta said, reaching down to
rub my shoulder but I ripped it away. "Melony still
has a lot of growing up to do first, and Lila had
already become so ill. She wouldn't have been able
to fight off an attack if it had come."

"But Parker has the powers now. Whether or not
Melony is okay, the Haberdash legacy is dead."

"That doesn't mean the people need to be," Greta
countered.

Connie, the well-dressed head of Commerce,
spoke up next. "By appointing someone outside of
her family, Lila knowingly destroyed her own line."

Greta's bright blue eyes flashed red. It startled
me so much, I kept my mouth clamped shut as the
others fought. "What choice did she have? People
are more important than power."

"The girl could have grown into the role," the
middle-aged guy who headed up Agriculture said.

"Or it could have destroyed her," Greta shot back, eyes still aflame.

"Enough!" Fluffikins shouted, and the fire in Greta's eyes disappeared. She took her seat beside me, and I moved to the opposite edge of mine, still completely unsettled.

"What now?" she asked calmly, sweetly—but I no longer took her good nature for granted. "Beech Grove needs its Town Witch."

All eyes turned to me. "I can't..." I sputtered.

"The magic we gave you was only temporary," the cat pointed out. "To become the official Town Witch, you'd need to kill your predecessor."

Parker's eyes found mine, and he stared at me as if seeing me for the first time.

"But Parker..." I mumbled.

"Yes, we're in a bad spot," Fluffikins admitted. "One person can't fill two roles indefinitely. It leaves the region too vulnerable."

"Then what are we going to do?" I cried, feeling beyond helpless. Rather than being resolved, things were only going to get worse. Would that mean more lives lost? I hated this.

"We'll have to find a new liaison to the Force, but the process takes a while, unfortunately," Fluffikins said.

"Usually we are better prepared for transitions, but Lila requested that we act fast and figure out the other details once the immediate threat had been mitigated."

"Can I help? You don't need me as a temp witch, anymore. Right? I can do the double cop thing." As scared as I was to be a part of this, it would be even worse to turn my back on them now.

"But you're not an officer," Parker said with a deadpan expression as he clenched his jaw.

"Can't you wave your magic wand and change the records?" I asked Greta since she was closest to me.

It was Fluffikins who answered for all of them. "We'd be even more vulnerable to have someone who hasn't been properly trained in either magic or policing in such a vital role."

"Then what? There must be something we can do!" I was on the verge of tears now. I hated that it made me look weak, but I was weak. Then again, if the strong ones weren't willing or able to fix the situation, doing so fell to me.

Parker stood suddenly, commanding everyone's attention. "Actually, I believe there is something. If you'll just hear me out..."

23

*P*arker barely spoke above a whisper. "I think there's a chance Melony could still be alive—badly injured and perhaps permanently wounded, but alive and well enough to call for reinforcements."

A memory swam to the front of my mind. While certainly menacing in our confrontation, Melony had also appeared frightened and desperate. If she'd wanted to hurt me or Greta, she could have easily done so while we were frozen in place.

But she hadn't.

She'd simply taken what she came for—*the old hat*—and left. She'd also asked Parker to surrender before mounting an attack, but what if he'd misread the situation? What if she hadn't meant to hurt him, either? What if we'd all gotten it wrong?

I bit my lip to keep from speaking out. Melony was already injured and possibly dead. It may be too late for anyone to help her, and there was also a very reasonable chance I was giving her way too much credit in this situation.

"You said she mentioned her grandfather when the two of you spoke," Fluffikins pointed out with a thoughtful tilt of his head. "Do you think they could be working together?"

My head spun with all the possibilities. Melony could be evil or she could be a scared kid, trying to impress the only family she had left. I certainly hadn't expected Parker to be Mrs. Haberdash's murderer—nor had I anticipated the fact that she'd been the architect of her own demise.

"Anything's possible, I suppose," Parker said in response to the boss cat, although his words felt as if they were specifically intended for me. Did he also suspect there was something more hidden just beneath the surface?

He cleared his throat and continued, "Even if she didn't survive, there's a chance he will still come looking for her... and then for revenge."

Fluffikins resumed his pacing. I realized he did

this whenever his thoughts moved faster than his words could. "Which puts us in a doubly vulnerable spot," he hissed, though it held no anger. "We're down a board member and may have to square off against a bonded enemy."

This new information cut my internal line of questioning short.

"What does that mean?" I asked, glancing from Parker to Fluffikins. "A bonded enemy?"

It was Greta who answered. "A grandfather and daughter—or any two blood relations, really— working toward the same purpose could amplify their magic through their family bond. It's like multiplying their powers rather than simply adding them together. So instead of 10 and 10 making 20, it makes 100. It's why some magic folk choose to have large families. They are practically unstoppable with so many bonds amplifying their powers."

"Most would use that bond only to protect themselves, but the Haberdashes..." Parker shook his head. "They've never been keen on following the rules."

"We have to find and stop them," I cried, my hesitation receding in light of this new information. "How can I help?"

"You can't," Fluffikins said with a deep frown that

pulled his whiskers toward his chest. "But the rest of us can ward the town as a protective measure just in case Melony's grandfather hasn't joined her yet. Do you still remember the power points?" he asked the rest of the board.

They all nodded solemnly. I took it they weren't talking about a computer program.

"I want to help, too," I insisted. "I still have magic. It may not be much, but maybe it will be enough to make a difference in whatever happens next."

"No, Tawny," Greta said in a cool, disconnected voice as she turned toward me. The fire had returned to her eyes, but it was only a dull flicker. I wouldn't have noticed it at all if she hadn't already been sitting so close.

She put a hand on my shoulder and pressed her forehead to mine. "It's very noble that you want to help, but this isn't your battle to fight. We've been protecting the magical interests in this region for years. Sometimes that includes stopping dangerous transfers of power. We're all trained for this..."

She grabbed both of my hands and pulled me to my feet with her.

I took a deep breath and waited.

Greta's eyes flashed, then returned to their normal blue color.

"We're all trained for this," she repeated. "But you're not."

With that last sentiment, she raised her other hand to my chest and ripped the magic brooch from my shirt.

My knees buckled, but I didn't fall despite feeling as if all the strength had been zapped from my muscles.

The pink glittery magic snapped out of sight as whatever power I'd briefly held within me fizzled and died. The silver brooch that held my borrowed magic glowed in Greta's hand. Taunting me. Practically daring me to take it back.

But I saw what power did. It turned answers into questions, loved ones into enemies, and safety into danger. Terrible things happened each and every day, and the board allowed them to happen as part of maintaining some kind of sacred balance.

But why did we need a balance at all? If I had magic, I'd use it to make a better world, not uphold a flawed and broken one.

Magic or not, I could still help.

Maybe because of my lack, I could help more. I could offer a human perspective.

"I'm not going anywhere," I said, standing firm.

But Greta shouted and gave me a mighty shove.

"Go! Return to your life and stop interfering with ours."

24

*O*f course, I now had a million questions flying through my brain, but before I could ask a single one, Greta shoved me again. And hard.

I struggled to see past her, hoping someone else would step in or speak up.

Parker studiously avoided my gaze.

Meanwhile Mr. Fluffikins summoned a blast of air so strong, it pushed me out into the empty hallway and slammed the conference room door behind me.

I landed on my rear with a heavy thump, just like I had last night when the bossy black cat had tested my magic by launching a sneak attack.

He'd said that if I'd had powers, I wouldn't be

able to stop the impulse to protect myself. If Greta ripping off my brooch hadn't been proof enough that my magic was gone, my failure to counter the attack certainly was.

The pain radiating from my backside added injury to insult.

I struggled to my feet and tried the doorknob, but it didn't so much as budge within my clammy grip. Stepping to the side, I pressed myself up against the glass-block column that looked into the room. "Let me in!"

I could hardly see more than shapes and movement past the 80s-tastic design feature, but even that was taken away when someone conjured a dark barrier to block my view

I stopped and listened.

Silence.

Had they also put up a sound barrier? Or had they all exited through that glass ceiling already?

Parker had mentioned power points, something about protecting the town from outside attacks. My guess was that wherever these points were, it wasn't inside the dingy office complex.

They were on the move—or at least they would be soon. I was out of options here, so I ran outside, wondering if I had any chance of following on foot.

Provided I was even able to spot them in the first place. I doubted both possibilities, given that my morning's journey on the magic broom had taken me well above civilian speed limits.

They needed my help. I knew that deep within my bones, even if they didn't. One way or another, I would find a way to—what was it Fluffikins had said?—to tip the balance.

Think, Tawny, think!

I knew Melony was either dead or in danger.

That her grandfather may also be involved, and if he was, that would be way worse than facing her by herself.

As the current holder of the town magic, Parker was at risk, too.

The board had discussed venturing to the power points to protect the town... And that's where my definite knowledge ended. Everything I knew about power points had more to do with making slide presentations than warding off dark magic. I had no car, and Greta had taken my magic away, both of which left me stranded in this mostly abandoned modern office complex.

So what now?

In the absence of a plan, I chose to head home. After all, there was only one place I thought might have the answers I needed, and that was Mrs. Haber-dash's house. I went there now, not because I was giving up, but because I knew that eventually the board and their foes would make their way back to where it all began.

And when they did, they would need me.

The house knew that, even if they didn't.

Why else would its magic have embraced me right away?

I found it especially strange that Greta had been the one to force me away. She'd seen the way the house opened up to me. She knew I was a part of this better than any of the rest of them did.

But they'd all been so quick to accept me into their group and even quicker to kick me to the curb. Why?

I slogged along the sidewalk, wishing I'd worn my running shoes so I could move a little faster to match the urgency of the situation.

I'd hardly made it around the block when a blast of burning light knocked me off balance and pushed me onto my poor sore bum once again.

Holding one hand over my eyes as a shield, I strained to see into the light. Was this a new enemy?

No, it was just Greta.

Okay, not *just Greta*.

It was Greta with enormous white wings stretched wide on each side. "Grab my hand," she ordered, and I knew better than to argue.

As soon as our fingers made contact, she launched back into the sky, pulling me along with her. "What's happening?" I managed to ask between frightened gasps for air.

"He's lying," she said with a quick glance my way. The flames had returned to her gaze, and she looked both beautiful and terrifying.

"What? Who's lying? And wait, are you a... an...?"

"Yes, I'm an angel, and Parker was lying."

Whoa. There was a lot to process there. I wanted to respond with something intelligent, but instead I just said, "Um, are you sure?" like some kind of mortal idiot... which I guess I was, considering the company.

"Almost everything he said was a lie, but I don't know why."

"So does that mean...?"

"Yes, Melony is fine. They never had a confrontation."

Finally I found some helpful words. "Then why didn't you stop everyone from going to ward the town?"

"Because something's not right. I didn't want to alert Parker to the fact I was on to him."

"How did you know he wasn't being honest?"

She pointed to herself and smiled. *"Angel."*

"Right."

"We need to act fast before he realizes that I haven't joined the others. Do you still want to help?"

She probably should have asked that before she catapulted me into the sky, but whatever. I was in this to win it, even though I had no idea how victory might look or what it would ultimately entail.

"Yes. I'll help. What do you need me to do?"

She flashed me a magnanimous smile that sent a shiver right through me. "You, my dear, are going to serve as our bait."

Wonderful.

25

"Where are we going?" I shouted into the wind as the angel and I picked up speed. "And how will I be used as bait?"

"We're going to the place where this whole thing started," Greta said as we zipped toward our location.

Not even a minute later, we clunked down right in front of Mrs. Haberdash's house, the place I'd been headed on my own, anyway.

"What's the plan?" I asked as Greta made her wings disappear with a quick flick of both wrists.

"Haven't really got much of one." She reached into her pocket and pulled out my brooch. Even though I hadn't been granted magic long enough to know what I was doing with it, I immediately felt relieved. If nothing else, my instinctual abilities could protect me—at least for a little while. I hated how much I wanted it, even though I was already beginning to suspect that magic did terrible things to a person's mind. Even knowing it could corrupt me, I wanted it. *Desperately.*

"It's a decoy," Greta explained, dashing my hopes just as quickly as she'd lifted them. Oh, well. It was definitely for the best. "Wear it. Pretend you're searching for something specific."

I thought about this for a moment. I also thought about how unfortunate it was that my pajama pants had no pockets. I shoved the decoy into my bra to keep it safe, then asked, "What should I be looking for?"

"Doesn't matter. Just tear around the house and generally make a nuisance of yourself. If one of the Haberdash heirs is around, they'll come find you." She stepped forward and I studied the back of her simple pastel pantsuit. There was no sign of the enormous wings that had delivered us to this location mere seconds ago. No tears from where they'd emerged through the fabric. No hint that she was anything other than an ordinary human being.

"What will you do?" I asked skeptically.

She glanced toward the horizon and frowned,

which was not exactly comforting. "I'll be watching from nearby, just as soon as I come back from informing Mr. Fluffikins of my observations."

Horror flooded my chest. "So I'll be alone in there?"

"Not for long, but I need to warn the others so they can be on the lookout. I know it's a lot to ask, but I promise to keep you safe. That's why I had to push you away. I couldn't let Parker know that I suspect him." She turned and stared off into the distance.

"You suspect Parker now? Of what?" Parker was the easiest for me to relate to on the board. I truly liked him, but I'd been wrong about people before.

Greta, for instance, had rubbed me wrong many times since I met her earlier that morning, but she also seemed the most genuinely concerned with what happened to me—and to Melony. Despite her warnings that magic always came to a violent end, it seemed she still yearned for a peaceful resolution here.

She worried her lip and brought her gaze back to meet mine. "I don't know, but it's not like him to lie. Back in the boardroom, didn't you notice that he seemed a bit, well... off?"

Actually I had, but I thought it was just because

of the trauma of potentially killing someone. I chose not to acknowledge that. I wanted to trust Greta, but I was still so confused about this brave new world of magic and danger. I mean, she was probably one of the good guys—being an angel and all—but how could I know for sure?

I suspected I wouldn't know anything for sure until it actually came to pass. Which meant my goal here was to find the truth and use it to guide my actions.

Oh, also to not die.

That was definitely important.

"You said you'd keep me safe. How can you guarantee that if you're not here?" I mumbled nervously.

Greta scanned the horizon again and shifted her weight from foot to foot before speaking. "Step forward," she instructed.

I did, and she grabbed my hand by the wrist, then placed it over my heart.

The blinding light shone again.

I blinked hard as I watched it pass from Greta's chest into my hand, up my arm, and then eventually into my chest, where the light faded and disappeared.

"You have my armor of light. It will be enough to keep you safe for the time I am gone," she said with a pained expression. Did it hurt her to lose this magic, the way losing mine had weakened me momentarily?

"What? I can't accept this. What about you?" I couldn't let her sacrifice herself like this. There had to be another way...

"I," she said with a wistful grin as she let out her wings again, "will just have to do my best not to die."

Before I could argue, she launched into the sky, leaving me to set my part of the non-plan into motion. And so I took a deep breath, rolled my shoulders like some kind of boxer prepping to go into the ring, and jogged up the porch steps to the empty house.

No, I didn't have any magical offenses, but I could still help somehow.

Greta believed in me enough to trust me with her very life, and I refused to let her down.

26

Greta had readily admitted she didn't really have a plan for us to follow. Neither of us knew for sure what was going on with Parker—or Melony for that matter.

Trouble was brewing, and we'd just have to deal with the resulting chaos as it came.

I couldn't offer much beyond my willingness to help, but that still might be enough to bait the bad guys... Um, whoever they turned out to be.

I thought about this more as I made my way upstairs to the late Mrs. Haberdash's bedroom. Greta had instructed me to pretend I was searching for something, and my performance would be far more convincing if I actually was trying to find something.

Melony had come for the old witch's hat earlier.

Might there be additional magical accessories just waiting to be discovered?

I thought of the decoy brooch nestled in my bra, and decided, yes. An accessory seemed a far better bet than trying to find some kind of revealing paper or book. Much more my style, too.

Maybe I'd get lucky and uncover something that could actually help. And if I didn't, that was also fine.

After all, I wasn't expected to actually find anything, just to create a distraction.

Greta hadn't given me much to go on—I suspected that was because she didn't know much herself—but she had revealed that Parker was lying to us. Could that mean Melony had already gotten to him and that he was now under her control? I remembered how helpless I felt when Parker and Fluffikins each took their turn manipulating my movements and emotions.

But how could Melony have overpowered someone like Parker? He was a much more experienced magic user, and he even had the town magic to bolster said powers even further. Not to mention, he had at least sixty pounds of muscle on her.

Granted, Melony had managed to hold both me and Greta when we had our confrontation earlier that morning, but maybe that was simply because she'd taken us by surprise.

Hmm. Now that I actually had more than a few fleeting seconds to think things over, I realized just how much wasn't adding up here.

Melony had surprised Greta and me at the house earlier that day. And when she left us, I ran to my house and found Fluffikins waiting. He conjured a broom and flew me back to the PTA complex with him. He'd also said Melony wasn't able to travel by magical means.

If that was the case, how could Melony have had the time to find Parker and follow him to the edge of town, have a talk, and then have a confrontation within that space of time before Parker joined us at the conference room table?

Yes, he was the last to arrive, but still we were only talking a span of maybe ten minutes here. For the first time since moving to this little town, I wished I'd brought a car with me. The town was considered tiny because of its population, but it still boasted a fair amount of land.

I punched my address into the maps app. Mrs. Haberdash's property—including my guest house— was centrally located, which made it easy to walk into town when I needed to. That had been a big selling point for me, actually.

Now that I was studying the map, I noticed we were dead center in the square-shaped area of the city's boundaries. I used my index finger to tap the city border and added it as a destination point. My app informed me that the quickest route by car would take about twelve minutes.

I didn't have exact timestamps for the events of this morning, but the accepted timeline seemed off.

Parker had either gotten confused or was purposefully lying to the board. Greta had already confirmed that.

But he'd also proudly told me he was a local, born and raised in Beech Grove. In fact, it was one of the first things he said to me—well, after accusing me of being a murderer, that is. I doubted he'd have made an error in calculating the time given his familiarity with the town, and I also doubted he'd tell a lie he knew could be easily disproved.

So why hadn't the others noticed this inconsistency?

Or had they but chosen not to acknowledge it?

I was missing something big here, and I doubted I was the only one.

See, this was exactly the kind of thing that

happened from making decisions too fast! Yet another reason it was so important for me to start my days with a slow, contemplative shower. Thanks to Fluffikins, I hadn't even gotten a quick and cold shower that morning.

I'd only had a single serving of coffee, too.

And it wasn't even eight o'clock yet. *Yawn.*

I rummaged through the late Mrs. Haberdash's jewelry box and lifted a large emerald ring to inspect it more closely.

"Drop that," someone ordered from the doorway in a gruff voice. Despite the added vitriol, I instantly recognized the speaker.

I turned to face Parker, holding the ring tight. "Make me," I challenged through clenched teeth. I was taking a big chance here and prayed my instincts were bang on.

He paused for a moment, but that was enough to confirm my suspicions.

"You're not Parker," I said, slipping the ring onto my finger and placing a hand on each hip in open defiance.

27

*P*arker unleashed a fiery blast and sent it careening right at me. Yeah, this definitely wasn't the same guy I'd met the day before.

I tried to dodge, but the surge of magic shot out so fast I didn't have a chance. The flames crashed straight into me, but I hardly felt a thing. Only warmth, acknowledgment. The light in my chest glowed as the borrowed angel armor absorbed the full impact.

"They know," Parker growled, and for a moment he looked too stunned to take any further action.

But that moment quickly passed and he hurled himself onto me, trapping my smaller body beneath his large, muscly one.

"Let me go!" I flailed against him.

"Tell me where the others are," he demanded, but still he couldn't force me to do it against my will. This wasn't Parker. He didn't have the same powers.

"No," I told him with another grunt. "I won't tell you anything until you explain who you are and what you want."

If I could get and keep him talking until Greta returned, then everything would be okay. I was definitely doing my job as bait. Now I just had to hope my fisherman would come to the rescue before the armor took one too many hits and I got gobbled up whole.

"Who are you? Why are you even a part of this?" fake Parker demanded rather than offering any answers of his own.

"I'm Tawny," I said blithely. The goal was to keep him talking, so if he wanted to hear about me, I was more than ready to offer up some info. "I'm just a temp."

"They took your magic and kicked you out. Why are you in this house? What are you looking for?"

I absolutely was not going to tell him that I was only here to distract him, so instead I reached for my writer skills and concocted a story—a bit of pure and simple fiction to save the day.

"I live in the guest house out back. When they

took my magic and kicked me out, I figured I'd been stiffed. I needed the money, though, that's why I even took the lousy job in the first place. Figured with everyone's attention focused elsewhere I could creep in here and find something to hock. Make sure I got some kind of payment for all my efforts."

"You made a bad choice," he hissed above me. "Because, see, now that you're here, I can't just let you go."

"Then let me help you," I suggested, giving up the struggle. The safest way to avoid getting hurt was to make him think I was on his side.

But it was to no avail. "I don't need help from a normie. This will be easier without you here to get in the way." He sent another surge of flames into my body, but I felt nothing this time. Just how long could this angel armor hold out? I really, really didn't want to find out.

"What's protecting you?" my attacker asked, further proof that he was not the Parker Barnes I knew and had even begun to care about a little.

"I don't know," I lied. I would have shrugged, but I still couldn't move beneath him. "Magical residue, maybe? As you said, I'm nothing but a normie. Please just let me go."

Another roar of ineffectual flames crashed against me.

"Use me as bait," I suggested in a squeaky voice. Panic had begun to set it. Would Greta make it back in time, or would the next blast be the one to break through my armor?

"What?" he asked, his hand lifted to conjure another blow, then paused.

"Don't just kill me. Use me as a bargaining piece for whatever it is you want." If I could be the bait for the good guys, then I could be the bait for the bad guys, too. Only Greta had the full picture. I had to trust that she would be back soon and make sure I escaped this scuffle alive. I mean, if you couldn't trust an angel, then who could you trust?

He pondered this for a few moments, and when at last he spoke again, it wasn't to me. "There you are. Now get in here, and help me tie her up," he said, pressing me harder into the ground. My face now lay flat against the heavy pile carpet in Mrs. Haberdash's bedroom.

The echoing footsteps paused just outside the doorway.

"Well? Were you able to incapacitate any of them?" fake Parker pressed.

"No, unfortunately. They went to the power

points as you anticipated, but they were unable to complete the ritual," a husky feminine voice answered.

I couldn't see much from my unfortunate position, but it was enough to recognize the pair of feet that joined us, dressed in thick black combat boots and a long flowy skirt.

Melony had arrived.

"Why not?" the man holding me down asked with a growl.

"One of their members suspected something and came to alert the others. I was just about to converge on the cat when it happened."

"What did she say? Come out with it already!" My attacker shoved me into the floor with all his might, but the angel armor held strong.

Melony drew closer but remained a couple steps back. "I couldn't hear, but the two of them took off together."

"They're going to warn the others. That means we don't have much time," the man said. "We have to finish this now. We might never get the chance again."

I swallowed hard.

Whatever came next, I knew it wouldn't be good.

28

"Why are you doing this?" I shouted, but my words got lost in the thick pile of the carpet. "What do you want?" I tried again, forcing the question from the side of my mouth.

"You think we wanted my stupid aunt's town magic? *Please*," Melony spat as she bound my wrists behind my back. "We've got much bigger fish to fry."

Well, at least she was keeping with the established metaphor, even if she hadn't exactly been let in on the whole thing.

"Melony, hush," the fake Parker scolded from where he was tying my ankles together.

She pulled back for a second before applying herself with even more vigor. "Sorry, Grandpa."

Oh, no. The family bond. This was exactly what Greta and the others had wanted to avoid.

Panic wrapped around my chest even tighter than my bonds. "Where's Parker? What did you do to him?" I mumbled again.

"He's dead," the Parker clone said with a laugh. "And soon you will be, too."

Oh, no. Were we really too late?

If they'd been able to kill Parker with his double dose of magic, then I didn't stand a chance. I was just one normal magic-less person up against two very magical people with an amplified family bond. I couldn't even get my hands or feet free to try to fight my way out of this or to make a run for it.

Would the other members of the board be able to defeat this villainous pair, or was the town of Beech Grove now doomed—and the entire region of Peach Plains right along with it?

A crash sounded from downstairs. Had my help finally arrived?

"Stay here," the fake Parker—Melony's grandfather—said. "I'll go investigate."

"Why are you doing this?" I asked the girl when the two of us were alone. "Is your life really so bad?"

"I don't have to answer that." She crossed her

arms over her chest but remained standing sentinel over me.

"Is this even something you want? Seems to me like your grandpa is the one calling all the shots. What makes you think he's going to share any of the magic he gains with you?" If I found the right words, perhaps I could sway Melony to my side. She'd had the chance to defeat me and Greta earlier, but she'd chosen not to. There had to be good in there somewhere.

She glowered at me. "Hush up. You don't know anything. Grandpa promised that if I help him with his plan, he'll make sure I take up my rightful place as Town Witch."

"If you say so," I responded casually.

She dug a heel into my back, but the armor of light held up, keeping me from feeling any of the pain. Okay, so maybe she was capable of inflicting some pain—but murder?

Everyone believed she'd come to town in order to kill her aunt, but what if they were wrong? What if Melony was after something else?

As we waited alone in that room, I turned Melony's last statement over and over in my mind. Her grandfather had said he'd make sure she became Town Witch.

As in future tense... As in it hadn't happened yet...

Which meant Melony *didn't* already have the town magic. Her grandfather wouldn't have killed Parker himself if he'd promised the magic to Melony. I still didn't know what they were after, but it was clearly something much bigger than the Beech Grove town magic.

They weren't after Parker. Perhaps they'd never been.

Chances were he was still alive.

Bigger fish to fry, Melony had said before her grandfather cut her off. Could I trick her into revealing more?

"What are you going to do with me?" I asked, turning slightly so it was easier to speak.

Melony's eyes met mine, and she flinched.

Perhaps she would have offered an answer, but I never got the chance to find out.

A strained cry rose from downstairs, silencing both of us.

Melony crept toward the door, and I remained on the floor, unable to do more than wriggle in place.

The next thing I heard was fake Parker shouting, "You're not going anywhere. Now march."

Melony ran out of the room to help, and I was able to move myself into a position that afforded me a better view of the doorway.

A minute later, the two of them strode in, pushing a burned and bloody Greta into the room before them. Without her angel armor to protect her, she'd been badly wounded by grandpa Haberdash's magical blows. She was barely conscious as they pushed her into the floor and tied her up as well.

She'd come to save me but had ended up in the line of fire herself.

Parker was missing, and the two of us had been captured. That left Fluffikins, Connie from Commerce, the old guy, and the slightly younger one who headed up Agriculture.

Would they be enough to stop Melony and her grandfather before they got their hands on whatever they were after?

Think, Tawny. Think!

If I couldn't unravel their plan, maybe I could still put a few chinks into it.

I didn't know how the family bond worked, but maybe I could still find a way to sever it.

Maybe I could still save the day.

No magic required.

29

"Where are the others?" Grandpa Haberdash kicked and barked at Greta, but his latest blow had rendered her unconscious and unable to answer. I hated seeing him use Parker's likeness to hurt us. No matter what happened after today, I knew I'd never be able to shake the image from my mind.

"They're coming. I just know it," Melony said, then worried her lip as she waited for her grandfather's acknowledgment.

He cracked his knuckles and scowled, not even looking at Melony as he said, "Stay put, and make sure these two don't cause any trouble. And do not under any circumstances leave this house. Do you hear me?"

Melony bobbed her head enthusiastically. "Yes, Grandpa."

And with that, her grandfather charged out of the room and down the long staircase. I listened but couldn't hear the door downstairs open or shut. My guess was that he had remained inside, lying in wait and ready to ambush whoever arrived next.

"So..." I wiggled onto my side so I could see Melony as I spoke. Perhaps her face would reveal something her words would not. I was fighting for my life here and had to use everything I had at my disposal. "Since we're both stuck here, want to tell me your master plan? I'm sure it's super smart."

She crossed her arms and looked away. "No."

Hmmm. If I couldn't appeal to her vanity, perhaps I could poke at her insecurities. I tried to shrug, but that didn't quite work considering my bonds. "I understand. I mean, we're both useless anyway. Might as well let the tough guys fight it out and tell us about it later."

Melony scoffed. "You may be useless, normie, but I'm not."

"Hey, why are you calling me a *normie?*" I tried to look hurt as I asked this. Vanity and insecurity hadn't worked, so what about humanity?

She rolled her eyes. "Because you don't have any magic, duh."

"Don't I, though? I'm the Town Witch."

She studied me for a moment, then shook her head. "No, the guy who killed my great aunt is."

"Maybe he's the official Town Witch, but as a temp for the PTA, I have an exact replica of the magic right here." I struggled against my bonds, then sighed.

She glanced back to me, uncertain. "Right where?"

"Well, I was instructed to keep the magic vessel close to my heart so that it would work best."

Melony took a step closer. "Where is it? Give it to me."

"I put it in my bra," I said with a grunt.

"That's gross."

"Well, do you want it or not?" I asked casually, trying to convey that it didn't matter to me if she accepted my help. A plan had started to form in my mind, though, and if I could get Melony to do her part, then Greta and I just might have a chance here. "I bet you'd be even more powerful than your grandpa if you had this extra jolt of magic. He wouldn't leave you on daycare duty then."

"Give it to me," she said again. Her eyes didn't

light on fire the way Greta's had, but I recognized a spark of greed.

I grunted and struggled against my bonds again. I had to make the show good. "I can't," I moaned, then flipped onto my back. The motion would have really hurt my tied-up wrists, but the angel armor was still protecting me from pain, thank goodness. I pressed out my chest as far as I could. "Come get it yourself. I can't exactly get it for you."

"Eeew, no." She sniffed in disgust and took a giant step back.

We both fell silent for the next couple minutes.

Neither of us moved until the sudden sound of a door banging open caused us both to jump in our skins.

"Last chance," I mumbled, trying hard to hide my desperation. "Take my magic and go be part of the action. I mean, if you're not there with him, how can you be sure your grandfather will even cut you in once he gets what he wants?"

Melony bit her lip again, then hurried over to my side. "I'll untie you for just a second, and just one hand. Give me the magic vessel, don't do anything funny, and I'll make sure you live. It's not like Grandpa and I have a use for you, anyway."

"Deal." I flashed her a relieved smile. Not

because she was offering me a way out, but because she'd fallen so perfectly into my trap.

I gave myself a quick mental pep talk as Melony struggled to untie just one hand. Downstairs, I heard Fluffikins shout, "Who are you, and what have you done with Parker?"

A series of crashes and slams followed as Melony used a fresh length of rope to tie my left wrist to the bonds that held my ankles before she finally got to work on freeing my right hand.

I was patient with her, like a good hostage.

"Okay, give it to me," she said when at last my hand was fully freed. I reached into my bra and found the decoy brooch Greta had entrusted to me. *Huh.* Who knew this thing would actually come in handy?

Melony accepted it greedily, wiping it off on the hem of her shirt before pulling it to her face for a closer inspection. She was too distracted by both the brooch and the action downstairs to immediately retie me, just as I had counted on.

While she studied the empty magic vessel, I brought my free hand back to my chest and pressed it against my heart, summoning the light within. It started small like a pinprick but then grew into a magnificent fruit-sized orb.

By the time Melony realized what I was doing, I had already thrust my hand toward Greta's unconscious body and allowed the light to flow out of me and into her.

The angel's eyes snapped open, full of white heat. I watched in awe as her wounds closed up and she regained full vitality.

Now that I no longer had her armor, I gasped as a sudden wave of pain crashed over me. The wrist that was still held captive behind my back had been twisted at an unnatural angle when I flipped myself onto my back. And when Melony had fastened it to my feet, that only made the break worse.

Yup, it was definitely broken.

Greta shouted beside me and ripped through the ropes that had held her.

"Go!" I urged in a hoarse whisper. "Take Melony out of here. Out of the... house."

I didn't see what happened next, because I passed out from the pain.

y head felt foggy. I heard hushed voices speaking around me but couldn't make out any of the words.

Ugh. How long had I been out? What day was it?

I'd had the craziest dream filled with talking cats, evil grandpas, and some kind of flaming angel. Well, that was one for the sleep journal. My therapist would love hearing about the story my nocturnal brain had concocted this time.

I brought my hands up to wipe the winkies from the corners of my eyes, then opened them.

A sleek black cat with a cute white patch on his chest stared down at me with glowing golden eyes. Huh, that was weird. When had I adopted a cat? I'd only lived in this town for a couple weeks, tops. I hadn't even unpacked all my boxes yet, but I'd gone out and adopted a pet?

Someone placed a warm hand on my forehead. Who was here with me? I was in my own room, not a hospital. Yet these people seemed to know me.

Fear sent my heart galloping full speed ahead as I turned and found a pale-haired woman wearing a simple pantsuit and a giant smile. "Oh, Tawny. I'm so glad you're okay."

I closed my eyes, took a deep breath, then opened them again. This time I spotted an incredibly handsome man with a salt-and-pepper beard and nicely toned arms standing behind the lady. His light gray eyes appeared curious—and also familiar somehow.

"May I have a moment with her?" he asked the others, who agreed and swiftly departed. Even the cat left. Wow, they really had him trained!

The handsome stranger sank down onto his knees and gripped my hand between his. "How do you feel?" he asked, concern reflecting in his pale eyes.

"Okay," I answered cautiously. It didn't seem like he wanted to hurt me, but what was he doing in my house while I slept? That was definitely kind of creepy. "Confused."

He glanced back toward the door. It was still shut.

"What do you remember?" he pressed, turning my hand over in his as if he couldn't quite believe it was real.

I tried so hard, but nothing came to mind. Just the weird dream and long, pleasant sleep. I knew my answer would disappoint him, but I also had no idea what to say in order to make him happy. Instead, I simply asked, "About what?"

He licked his lips and tried again. "What's my name?"

"I don't know. Is it Steve? You look like a Steve." I smiled to soften the blow in case I got it wrong. Even though this man was a stranger to me, *he* clearly knew *me*.

The man hung his head and chuckled. When he looked back at me, I thought I caught the glimmer of a tear that refused to fall.

"Forgetting is the protocol," he said, making me even more confused than before. "I mean, it's the *usual* procedure." He shrugged.

I furrowed my brow but said nothing. What could I say? *Hey, crazy guy. I have no idea what you're taking about. Get out of my bedroom!*

He continued on, undeterred. "But, Tawny, there is nothing usual about you."

"Who are you?" I asked. My throat felt dry. My head foggy. None of this was making any sense.

He waved his hand in a semi-circle, then flicked his index finger straight up, watching me the whole time.

"Who am I?" he prompted again. "Think, Tawny. You know this."

And suddenly the fog lifted, revealing images from the past day and a half. Fluffikins sharing his memories with me as he purred on my lap, Greta propelling me through the air with strong and steady wings, that old guy in the suit whose beard reached down to his belt buckle, but more than anything... the man standing right before me.

I couldn't stop the enormous smile that blossomed on my face. "You're Parker."

"And what do you last remember happening?"

A frightening vision filled my mind. We'd almost been defeated. A horrible pain. I passed out.

"Melony and her grandfather," I said, trying to slow the swirl of images as I spoke. "They were in Mrs. Haberdash's house. Said they had bigger fish to fry. That you were dead. Greta gave me her armor of light, but then I gave it back. Did she get Melony out of the house?" That had been the last thing I'd said before losing consciousness—to get Melony out of there—based on a sneaking suspicion I had that somehow the house amplified their family bond that much further. But had I been correct?

Parker raised my hand to his lips and gave it a lingering kiss. "Yes, you were right about everything. The moment Greta vaulted through the window with Melony in her grasp, the connection broke and the others were able to overpower her grandfather."

"But why?" I knew Melony's grandfather had urged her not to leave the house, but I still didn't understand the full extent of it.

"Simple," Parker said with a crooked grin. "Lila Haberdash lived her entire life in that house. Her parents lived there before her, and their parents before them. Over time, the house has absorbed generations of family magic—so much so that it became a part of them."

"And it amplified their bond," I said, finally understanding.

He nodded and looked as if he wanted to say something else, but I still had more questions that needed to get out of me.

"What were they after? Why did they need that extra power if Mrs. Haberdash was already dead?"

"They were never after her. At least the grandfather wasn't." He took a deep breath and squeezed my hand before letting it go. "They wanted the board."

"Who? Fluffikins?"

"Yes. And Connie. And Greta. And Buckley. And—"

"All of you." I exhaled slowly, taking this new information in. If Melony and her grandfather had been successful, they could have destroyed the magical balance completely. Could have done whatever they wanted with all that power, no matter how horrible.

Parker nodded, confirming my suspicions. "We are the strongest in the region. If they were able to assume all our power for themselves, they'd be unstoppable. They thought with Lila out of the way, they could use the house to help accomplish that."

"But they failed."

"They failed. Thank goodness for that." Parker looked so tired now. Was that because he'd been worried about me? How long had I been out? How badly had he been hurt?

"Where were you?" I asked gently.

Luckily, he didn't seem to take offense. "Incapacitated," he stated simply.

"Oh." I decided not to press further. Instead I

switched back to the previous topic, "So their whole plan hinged on everyone coming to the house?"

"Since it was a major source of their power, yes. But they were also counting on us coming one by one, so we'd be easier to defeat. That's why Melony's grandfather took my form, so he could sway our actions. He dropped just enough hints to raise suspicions, then sent us to the power points in order to divide us."

This all made sense, but it didn't complete the puzzle. Not yet. "But they didn't kill me or Greta when they had the chance. Why?" This more than anything, I needed to know.

Parker shrugged and pressed his lips together in a tight line. "I don't think Melony ever quite understood the full extent of her grandfather's plan. I don't think we do, either."

"What happened to him?"

"Fluffikins dropped him off in the farthest possible region from here. New Zealand, I think."

"But he'll be back." This wasn't a question, because I already knew for sure it would happen.

"Yes. This time we'll be expecting him, though."

"What happens now?"

"The board will find a new Liaison to the Force, and I'll work at filling Lila's very big shoes as Town

Witch. You go back to living your normie life. Hope-fully, though, you'll be up for frequent visits from your new landlord and friend?"

"I'd like that," I said, feeling like an old-timey movie heroine. Now would have been the perfect time for Parker to sweep me off my feet—or rather my bed—and give me that sweet and perfect first kiss.

Instead, he leaned forward and hugged me tight, then whispered in my ear, "This will be our little secret. Okay?"

"My lips are sealed. Well, on one condition," I whispered back.

"Anything," he promised. He also wouldn't stop smiling.

"Would you please fix my hot water heater before you go? I could really use a nice long shower."

Think Tawny's magical adventures with the PTA have come to an end? Not a chance...

CLICK HERE to get your copy of *Psychic for Hire* so that you can keep reading this series today!

And make sure you're on Molly's list so that you hear about all the new releases, monthly giveaways, and other cool stuff (including lots and lots of cat pics).

You can do that here:
MollyMysteries.com/subscribe

WHAT'S NEXT?

After my last assignment almost killed me, I thought I was done with the Paranormal Temp Agency. Turns out we were just getting started...

The board of paranormal liaisons is down a member, leaving Beech Grove vulnerable to outside magical influence. Worse still, the stray cats who work as our field agents are disappearing from the streets—and they're not winding up in shelters.

Now my boss, a black cat named Mr. Fluffikins, has ordered me to go undercover as a phony psychic and find out what's happening to the missing feline agents.

Last week I didn't even know magic existed; this week it's up to me to help save it.

Yup, all in a day's work for this part-time psychic.

PSYCHIC FOR HIRE is now available.

CLICK HERE to get your copy so that you can keep reading this series today!

SNEAK PEEK OF PSYCHIC FOR HIRE

My name's Tawny Bigford. I'm a 35-year-old part-time romance author, and I just found out that magic is real.

You see, it all started one morning when I stumbled upon my new landlady's dead body. From there I was whisked away by a dashing cop who wasn't exactly there to investigate her murder. He delivered me to the PTA—no, not the one you're thinking—the Paranormal Temp Agency.

They're the special governing body that protects magical interests in our fair Peach Plains region of Georgia and are one of many such boards set up all across the globe.

Once they determined I was not at fault for my landlady's death, they ordered me to act as her temporary replacement. Not as a landlady, but as the official Beech Grove Town Witch. Oh, boy!

From there it was all talking cats, flying brooms, and one twisty turn after another. Every time someone actually bothered to answer one of my questions, at least a dozen more popped up in its place.

By the time we caught the real killer on the loose, I had a terrible headache from trying to keep it all straight. Here's what I do know...

The board is made up of six paranormal liaisons plus the Town Witch and the assigned Diplomat in charge. Our Diplomat is a little black cat who loves following rules almost as much as he loves making demands; his name is Mr. Fluffikins.

Then we have sweet, matronly Greta as the liaison to Schools. I recently found out she's an angel —um, wow!

Parker Barnes is that same cop who initially brought me into this crazy supernatural ring. He's also the reason I remember everything that happened even though the others attempted to wipe my memory. Beyond that, his role is a bit more complicated. I'm still trying to figure it out for myself.

Lastly, we have Connie in charge of Commerce,

Buckley as head of Agriculture, and some old dude in a suit who serves as the emissary for Cemeteries.

I was recently the temporary Town Witch, but now that they have someone more permanent to fill the role, I should be out of a job. The board works with temps for a reason. They're easier to control, and the fewer people who know the full truth about what they do, the better. They'd rather tell lots of people part truths than let anyone too deep into their circle and risk exposure. I guess that's why I find them so confusing.

Even though I'm a little sad to have lost the magic they granted me—I only had it for less than twenty-four hours, mind you—I'm more than ready to get back to my normal life.

The boss cat, however, seems to have other ideas...

Uh-oh.

It's been three days since the madcap magical adventure that changed my world and everything I knew about it. Three days since yet another cold shower led to a murder mystery that turned into a magical conspiracy that almost cost me my life.

Three days.

That's longer than the entire adventure lasted. I

don't even think a full twenty-four hours passed between the time when I stumbled over Mrs. Haberdash's corpse and the PTA board caught the bad guys and put a stop to their dastardly plan.

In fact, I know it wasn't.

So how can such a short span of time change literally everything?

For one thing, I have a new landlord now. And while my previous landlady Mrs. Haberdash studiously avoided me, Parker Barnes finds at least half a dozen excuses to stop by every single day.

Yes, *that* Parker.

It's kind of hard to push magic out of my mind when the same guy who introduced me to it in the first place is always hanging around my doorstep.

And it definitely doesn't help that I have a big fat crush on him. Ever since my ex-husband found a new wife—while we were still married, I might add—I've sworn off love for a life of complete personal freedom.

So while Parker's swoony gray eyes may make my heart gallop, they also make my stomach churn. That's why I've imposed three new rules.

Three days. Three rules.

They are no more magic, no more men, and no more madcap adventures.

That was it. Should've been easy enough to follow. Especially since the rest of the board assumes I have no recollection of what happened.

But then...

Crash!

I jumped out of bed and ran down the hall as fast as my feet would carry me. Too late I realized that I probably should have found some kind of weapon to take with me.

It was hardly six in the morning. Who could have possibly...?

A spark of light flooded the living room even though I hadn't flipped the switch.

"Good morning, Tawny," Mr. Fluffikins said from where he was seated right beside a broken vase that had once held an arrangement of fake flowers. I didn't have the money to constantly buy fresh, and I hated watching something so pretty and vibrant wilt and die, so it had always been fake for me.

I glanced from the mess to the cat who had no doubt created it and back again, then threw my hands in the air and headed back down the hall toward my bedroom.

"Tawny, wait!" he cried after me. "I know you remember!"

I mumbled my three rules to myself. Fluffikins's

appearance threatened to break at least two of said rules, and that was not okay.

"Go away," I mumbled and continued to drag myself back toward bed.

"I won't," he insisted, trailing after me now. "Not until you at least hear me out."

"I'm not making you breakfast." The last time he appeared at my place before sunrise that's what he had demanded. It was a safe bet that's what he wanted now.

"I already ate," he countered. "And you clearly haven't forgotten anything despite the fact I very clearly remember wiping your memory."

This stopped me dead in my tracks. I shuddered and then asked, "What do you want then?"

"The PTA has a new assignment for you," he said, and then my knees gave out beneath me.

PSYCHIC FOR HIRE is now available.

CLICK HERE to get your copy so that you can keep reading this series today!

ABOUT MOLLY FITZ

While USA Today bestselling author Molly Fitz can't technically talk to animals, she and her doggie best friend, Sky Princess, have deep and very animated conversations as they navigate their days. Add to that, five more dogs, a snarky feline, comedian husband, and diva daughter, and you can pretty much imagine how life looks at the Casa de Fitz.

Molly lives in a house on a high hill in the Michigan woods and occasionally ventures out for good food, great coffee, or to meet new animal friends.

Writing her quirky, cozy animal mysteries is pretty much a dream come true, but sometimes she also goes by the names Melissa Storm and Mila Riggs and writes a very different kind of story.

Learn more, grab the free app, or sign up for her newsletter at **www.MollyMysteries.com**!

PET WHISPERER P.I.

Angie Russo just partnered up with Blueberry Bay's first ever talking cat detective. Along with his ragtag gang of human and animal helpers, Octo-Cat is determined to save the day... so long as it doesn't interfere with his schedule. Start with book 1, *Kitty Confidential*.

PARANORMAL TEMP AGENCY

Tawny Bigford's simple life takes a turn for the magical when she stumbles upon her landlady's murder and is recruited by a talking black cat named Fluffikins to take over the deceased's role as the official Town Witch for Beech Grove, Georgia. Start with book 1, *Witch for Hire*.

SPECIAL COLLECTIONS

Black Cat Crossing
Pet Whisperer P.I. Books 1-3
Pet Whisperer P.I. Books 4-6
Pet Whisperer P.I. Books 7-9
Pet Whisperer P.I. Books 10-12

CONNECT WITH MOLLY

You can download my free app here:
mollymysteries.com/app

Or sign up for my newsletter and get a special digital prize pack for joining, including an exclusive story, *Meowy Christmas Mayhem*, fun quiz, and lots of cat pictures!
mollymysteries.com/subscribe

Have you ever wanted to talk to animals? You can chat with Octo-Cat and help him solve an exclusive online mystery here:
mollymysteries.com/chat

Or maybe you'd like to chat with other animal-loving readers as well as to learn about new books and giveaways as soon as they happen! Come join Molly's VIP reader group on Facebook.

mollymysteries.com/group

MORE PEACH PLAINS PARANORMAL

Welcome to the paranormal world of Peach Plains.
It's a rural region of Southern Georgia where magic
is real and mysteries abound. If you loved this book,
make sure to check out its sister series from other
talented authors...

View them all and grab links here:
www.SweetPromisePress.com/paranormal

Paranormal Temp Agency
by Molly Fitz

Tawny Bigford's simple life takes a turn for the magical when she stumbles upon her landlady's murder and is recruited by a talking black cat to take over the deceased's role as official Town Witch. Tawny didn't even know magic existed in the real world, but now she's expected to use her newly granted powers to catch a killer and stop a deadly chaos from taking over the town.

The Secret Academy
by Mila Riggs

Nestled among the hills and forests of Winding Creek, Georgia, the Secret Academy lies hidden in plain sight. It's an exclusive school for the world's most powerful young magic users... and also Zoey Harper. Unfortunately, this strange new world Zoey finds herself in doesn't come with a rulebook or a map, but it does come with a captive white tiger who's decided to stick to her like glue. Meanwhile, nobody's seen her particular magical gift for decades, which means they're all watching and waiting to see whether she'll use her abilities to better their world or to tear it apart from the inside. No pressure, right?

The Magical Soapmaker Mysteries
by SE Babin

Moonmist Springs is home to Georgia's most magical new soap shop, The Suds Stop. Its owner, Ivy Bradshaw is not exactly a witch... but also not exactly human. When a missing box of lye from her store gets linked to a recent small-town murder, everyone assumes she's the one to blame. Luckily, she has a talking skeleton and the world's most adorable pup to help with her amateur sleuthing. But will this ragtag trio be able to identify the real killer before Ivy's once sparkling-clean reputation is dirtied beyond hope?

The Magical Real Estate Mysteries
by Carolyn Ridder Aspenson

Travel to Swan Hollow, Georgia, magic is everywhere and ghosts are real. As the one and only full-time assistant to a part-time real estate agent, Alyssa Grey does it all. She delivers contracts, picks up dry-cleaning, and occasionally even gets to help show the old houses her boss specializes in listing. Old houses, of course, come with lots of extra work to do. Will Alyssa be able to dispose of the skeletons in the closets and settle the disrupted ghosts who haunt the halls in time to make the sale? There's more at stake than a few hundred thousand dollars here—getting it wrong could cost Alyssa her magic... or her life.

Bewitching the Rich Guy
by Michelle Francik

Welcome to Greveswood, Georgia, home to sweet tea, succulent peaches, and the country's hottest new reality dating show. When Stella Spinney learns it will be filmed in the infamous Marwood Manor, she enlists the help of her three best friends to infiltrate the competition and discover the truth about the stolen estate that was meant to be her family legacy. With this club of Four Rich Witches on the case, the other competitors don't stand a chance... especially when they find out they'll be solving a murder or two while locked in together with no hope of escape. Yikes! Who cares about the guy when there is so much more at stake? Oops, maybe Stella kind of likes him after all.

Channeling Ghosts for Beginners
by Izzy Wilder

Fiddlehead Creek is a strange place to live, and hapless psychic-in-training Esme Hightower is among the strangest of its residents. These days, she's just a few satisfied clients away from a big promotion. Unfortunately, most of her latest readings involve solving murders while attempting to sidestep pesky ghosts. Despite the added attentions of a very persistent—and very annoying —shape-shifting hunk, Esme needs to keep her head on straight or risk losing everything she's worked so hard for. That is, if she can survive long enough to expose the killer and bring justice to the dead.

Once Upon a Witch
by Nyx Halliwell

Once upon a time in a small Georgian town called Story Cove... Four magical sisters with extraordinary witchy powers find themselves in very real, living versions of their favorite fairytales. These stories come with princes and castles, but also murder, mystery, and—let's not forget—magic. Enchantment abounds as they fight evil, break curses, and navigate the modern dating world, all while searching for their personal happy endings. But can they do it before reaching THE END?

Roots of Magic
by Mila Riggs

There's no place quite like Elyria, Georgia. This

quiet farm town is hiding a dangerous secret. Magic is real and very much necessary to their quaint way of life. So what happens when a powerful being from a far-off land accidentally finds herself lost among them? Could it be the end of magic as they know it? And just what are they willing to sacrifice to avoid losing it forever?

Dark Gifts
by Mila Riggs

The boring South Georgia town of Grandon Township is about to get a whole lot more interesting, thanks to a new psychic shop that's just opened up down the road. Now local teens are finding themselves with extraordinary powers, and they'll need help to control their newfound abilities. Among the first to present is Alex Kosmitoras, a blind sophomore who gains the ability to "see" the future. The fates sure were having fun when they came up with that one. But will he be able to use his other senses to interpret his haunting visions and save a close friend from dying what seems a certain death? That's one answer he doesn't have, and it may be the only one that matters.

View them all and grab links here:

www.SweetPromisePress.com/paranormal

Made in the USA
Monee, IL
06 November 2020